The Roles We Own

(Artists and Athletes book 4)

By CD Rachels

The Roles We Own (Artists and Athletes Book 4)

Cover Illustration Copyright © Story Styling Cover Designs
Professional beta read by Catherine at Les Court Services. www.lescourtauthorservices.com
Copy Editing by Karen Meeus. www.karenmeeusediting.com

Omar

Romance isn't for me. Don't get me wrong, I love the corniness of rom-coms, but it's not in the cards in my life. I play hard on the soccer field, I party hard with my boys, and I fool around with any girl or guy who's hot and willing. The only person off-limits: my best friend's boyfriend's brother, Sly O'Rourke. He's cute, but I don't do feelings.

Staying away from him would be easy if I didn't have to direct the school musical for my degree credits. Sly is auditioning, and he's not the shy, nerdy dude everyone thinks he is. He's talented, charming, and gorgeous—totally boyfriend material, if I'd ever do relationships. When he asks for help practicing physical intimacy for the play, how can I refuse? It's my job to make sure this musical is a success, and that's what this is: strictly business.

But when his mouth catches mine, our bodies don't get the memo. I don't think Sly and I are acting anymore.

Sly

I've played the role of a comfortable straight guy for too long. The truth is: the thought of physical intimacy makes me nauseous. I'm not interested in anyone, guy or girl, which sucks, because I've always wanted a romantic story of my own.

Now that I'm at Korham University, I have the chance to redefine myself. If I play the role of a romantic hero during the semester musical, maybe I'll learn to enjoy touching people or catch real feelings for once. There is one complication to my plan: I have to spend a lot of time with soccer jock Omar Odom. He's a touchy, handsy, party boy, but I eventually see a different side to him. As the weeks go by, my brother's boyfriend's best friend doesn't seem so bad. He's chill in ways I never could be and supports me in the play. He's the perfect guy who can help me with the physical aspects of the dramatic arts.

When Omar puts his mouth on mine, I expect to be repulsed, not burning up on the inside. I've never wanted a girl or guy before so...what is happening to me? And why don't I want it to stop?

["The Roles We Own" is a low-angst, male/male romance about new adults in college. It involves theater rehearsals, soccer games, frat parties, cartoon onesies, raisin bagels, and discovering what gray-asexuality can mean.

It is the fourth book in the *Artists and Athletes* series but can be read as a stand-alone.]

To J. Thanks for teaching me soccer lingo for this book. Oh, and for loving and marrying me.

1: Omar

"Romance is a sham." I lean forward so my new best friend, the cab driver, can hear me from the backseat. "Did you know that? Romance as a concept was invented a millennium ago to justify the nuclear family who had to work on ancient farms. Then later, it was peddled to give our boys something to look forward to while at war overseas. Then it was greeting cards, chocolates, and Drew Barrymore movies. Which brings us to the present, with apps on apps selling the prospect of digital love. But all of it is a lie."

He doesn't respond. I want to keep riding the warmth coursing through my veins, so I continue, "I just got back from a frat party where I got freaky in some girl's room, and she wanted me to stay. But you wanna know what I said?"

I'm met with silence. "I said I had to go study. Because I didn't want her catching feelings or anything like that. We varsity soccer boys get plenty of groupies, so it's part of the jock lifestyle. But it's better not to let anyone get attached to me because I'll hurt them down the line. Strings lead to

1

expectations, which only lead to let-downs—relationships hurt, man." The cab ride is making me feel dizzy, with streetlights piercing through the darkness of the night. I want to drink more, but I don't reach for the bottle of vodka in my over-the-shoulder fanny pack. Taking a shot right now would be wrong on so many levels—I'm drunk, but I'm still ethical.

"As a matter of fact," I continue, "one of my best friends, Landon, fell hard last semester, but now? He's moping in his dorm room, I'm sure, because the dude—I mean, the *person*— broke things off with him during the summer. Apparently his special person is taking a sabbatical from college for some dance internship in New York City. Anyway, heartache is real, yes. But romance?" I shake my head way too aggressively. "Doubtful at best."

"What about your parents?" my driver asks. We pass a stoplight as we encroach on the Korham University campus. "Are they married?"

"Mhm. Okay, sure, my parents love each other, I think, but they got married because my grandparents expected it." I swallow back a burp. "You're a good guy. What did you say your name was again?"

"Muhammed, sir." His thick white mustache bounces as he talks, and his glasses reflect the campus lights.

"Nice to meet you, Muhammed." My speech is starting to slur, but I don't care because I'm enjoying this conversation. "You from Bangladesh? My parents are from Bangladesh. Don't let my lighter complexion fool you. I'm definitely their son."

"Pakistan, sir." He pulls up to the curb near a cluster of dormitories.

"Ah. You're a good man." I smile and pat his shoulder. "It

was nice chatting with you. I'll give you a nice tip on the app."

"Thank you, sir." He turns to me. "And Omar? I'm sorry for whoever hurt you."

I'm stunned sober and silent for a moment. There's no way he knows about my past. A moment later I'm back to grinning. "Ahhh, you're alright, Muhammed!" I laugh and stumble out of the cab.

I grip my fanny pack tightly on my shoulder as I walk up the stairs, eyes half-lidded at this point. It's past one a.m. on the Saturday before classes start, and I expected more college kids to be wandering about. Instead, I'm all alone as I approach my building. Once at the door, I frisk myself for my key card, but it's not on me. I unzip my pack—just a bottle of vodka, no ID card. *Shit*, I must have dropped it when I was fleeing what's-her-name's room while putting my pants on.

I look around and see no one's here to let me in. Crap. Now I'm locked out of my own damn dorm. Two of my best friends, Ravi Metta and Landon, now live in an off-campus apartment. They'd let me crash there, but it's like a twenty-minute uphill walk. My third best friend, Kareem Hall, lives with me, but he's sleeping over at his girlfriend's tonight. Why didn't I get the phone numbers of the other soccer players that live in our suite?

Ah well. These things happen. I walk back down the stairs toward the main quad, gripping my precious bottle of vodka. Oh alcohol, you can be my best friend tonight, second only to Muhammed.

I find what I'm hoping is the comfiest bench on campus and take a seat under a streetlamp. After a few more swigs of delicious hard liquor, I feel the sleepiness start to take me. I reflect on how Landon is going through heartbreak, but Ravi and Kareem are living their best lives with their boyfriend and girlfriend, respectively. I don't want to be hurt like Landon, never again, so I refuse to be jealous of Ravi or Kareem. It's my senior year of college, and I'm a bisexual varsity soccer player; I need to live it up, and catching feelings isn't in the cards for me.

"Cheers to another year of being single," I say out loud to the darkness around me. I take another big sip. "And loving it."

As I lie down, the bench feels so cozy I feel myself swiftly falling into dreamland.

2: Sly

I walk out of the campus library clutching the novel I've decided to borrow. It's late at night, but even with my glasses on, I see no one around me. Good. I don't want anyone to judge me for taking out a pulpy romantic comedy book, or a rom-com as the fans call it.

It's just that romance is the *best*—the genre, anyway. The dramatic confessions, the corny plots, the slow dancing, the tender kisses—whether in books, movies, or plays, I love it all. It's ironic because I've never had a girlfriend since the thought of intimacy doesn't appeal to me.

Haphephobia is the irrational fear of being touched, which, according to my research, is separate and different from being asexual. I won the shitty lottery of life by being both.

I want so badly to have a perfect kiss, but being that close to someone has always made me grossly uncomfortable. I long to feel those sparks with the right girl. I'm just not wired that way, and it scares the crap out of me. I feel like I'm destined to be lonely forever because I can't find a person who makes dating worth it. Even if I did, who would want to spend their time with someone who's afraid of a simple kiss or hug?

I think that's why I love romance as a genre. I get to live vicariously through heroes who actually enjoy kissing and sex. With enough rom-com exposure, maybe I can learn to be like these guys and get over my stupid fear of physical contact.

I get in my car and buckle my seatbelt. After taking off my glasses, since I only really need them when I'm reading, I back up out of a parking spot. My first Saturday night at a big university like Korham, and I'd spent it at the library reading books.

Sly O'Rourke, you daredevil, if you keep living life on the edge like this, you might get a papercut.

Admittedly, the huge selection of books at the library is part of the reason I came to KU. My brother Steven would give me so much grief if he knew that, but he's so wrapped up in his boyfriend Ravi he won't notice. I transferred here after two years of community college, and I'm thrilled to be living away from my parents for the first time.

As I drive around the quad, I spot one person — presumably a drunk dude sleeping on a bus stop bench. Slowing down, I realize I recognize him; my brother is dating the soccer captain, and this guy is definitely part of his posse. I've seen this guy, with his light-brown skin and objectively handsome face, in Steven's social media pictures.

This jock would kick my ass if he knew I thought he was handsome, but it's not like I have a crush on him. He simply has features most people consider appealing and a nice physique. I use those terms to describe the cast of *New*

Girl. It doesn't mean I'm sexually or romantically interested in any of them.

Hell, it would be easier if I was clearly interested in guys. That'd be a less lonely existence than not being into anyone; life sucks for someone who's probably asexual but craves companionship.

I park at the curb and walk up to Rip Van Winkle over here. What was his name again...Kareem? He's clinging to a bottle of liquor and looks like he's had one too many. Shit, I can't leave him out here. He could get expelled if he's caught. Worse, he could hurt himself.

"Psst. Hey, you. Soccer guy." I shake his shoulder, and, to his credit, he wakes up.

"Mmm...hey! Hey, it's you!"

"Huh?" I ask while he sits up. His eyes are red, and his eyelids keep fluttering up and down.

"Steven! You fffffound me..." He almost falls over again, and I prop him up.

"Not Steven. Are you okay, Kareem?"

"You know I'm not Kareem, Steven." He giggles and puts his hand on my shoulder. "I'm Omar!"

I flinch away at first, then remember he's really drunk. Ravi or Landon, my other suitemate are gonna have to take care of him, so it's a good thing I live with his soccer buddies.

"Sorry, Omar. Come on, you can sleep back at my apartment. Ravi and Landon are there." I point to my car, and, fortunately, he walks by himself. He gets in and he falls asleep immediately after I help him with the seatbelt. I'll take that as a win.

I drive the ten minutes to our school-sanctioned

off-campus apartment. Upon arrival, I once again have to wake up Omar.

He springs to life, and I lead him out of the car. "Thanks, Steven. You're so…chivalrous…and handsome." He strokes my face, and for a moment, I let him. It's a gentle caress, and his hand feels nice on my face, which is pleasantly surprising. "Sorry, I forgot you're 100 percent property of Ravi." Remembering what's happening, I pull away.

"I'm not Steven," I say, irritated. I remind myself he's drunk and that my brother and I do look similar sometimes.

"It's okay, Steven," he says, slurring his voice. "I don't believe in romance or feelings anyway. It's just…not in the cards for me."

Huh. I file away that little piece of trivia for later. I need to focus on the task at hand, helping to house someone who's basically a stranger. *I'm doing the right thing, I'm doing the right thing…*

We make it up the stairs and into my apartment without Omar waking up anyone. I live with my brother, his boyfriend, and their soccer buddy Landon. Once inside, the lights are off, and the others all seem to be asleep. "You can sleep on the couch."

"Thanks, Steven." I once again don't even bother to correct him. I find a trash bucket and put it next to him.

"I'll be in my room, Omar. Here's a bucket for—" He wretches, and I turn away. Perfect timing.

After he's done spewing his stomach, Omar falls right back asleep. I get a bottle of water, put it next to him on the couch, and toss over a Korham University blanket we have lying around. Ravi and Landon *totally* owe me big time for looking out for their drunk teammate.

Still, seeing him lying here safe and sound, it's nice to feel useful. Solving human problems and social issues —that's what life has always been about for me, and Omar clearly has his share.

And hell, I didn't completely freak out when he stroked my cheek, so that's a win. I want so badly to be comfortable enough to let anyone touch me. Part of the reason I've come to KU is to broaden my horizons and push myself out of my comfort zone. Maybe Omar caressing my cheek—with his warm fingers and perfect face—is a sign I can be a normal college student after all.

Curling up in my bed, I replay the feeling of Omar touching me. It wasn't awful at all, unlike almost every other physical contact I've ever had—no, it was actually really nice.

3: Omar

I wake up in a suite that's not mine. Where am I? Did I pass out in some hook-up's dorm, again? I'm usually so diligent at getting off and making a getaway.

No, I recognize this place. This is Ravi's and Landon's apartment. They share this with Steven and...Did he bring me here last night?

"You're a hot mess, you know that?" Ravi walks by wearing only pajama pants. He gets out a bowl from a cupboard in their kitchen area and starts pouring some cereal. "You're lucky one of us found you. He said you were clinging to a bottle of vodka like a baby clings to milk." He gives me an unimpressed look, and I sit up and shake my head.

Wow, should *not* have done that; now the room is spinning. "Well, they're both good sources of calcium," I mutter, grabbing the water and taking a gulp. It rids my mouth of the taste of liquor and I'm already feeling better. I slowly get up to join Ravi in the kitchen nook. "I need to thank your boyfriend for housing me. What was he doing out so late?"

"Steven didn't bring you back here. Sly did."

"Who?" I open up all their cupboards and finally find the porcelain bowls.

"Steven's brother." He munches on some cereal and my eyebrows jump.

Oh. A lot of things about last night make sense now.

"Shit, I didn't even know he had a brother. Are they twins?" I swipe the cereal and pour myself a bowl.

"Sly's a year younger. Milk's in the fridge, but don't touch the almond milk. That's Sly's and he doesn't want our jock cooties."

I chuckle and sift through the fridge. "I'll need to thank him. I'm pretty sure I lost my ID card and decided to take a nap on a park bench."

"Yeah, he told me. He dragged you here and tucked your drunk ass in on our couch. You better not pull this shit during the season."

"Okay, *mon capitaine*," I reply with a fake French accent, rolling my eyes. I pour the milk into my bowl and Ravi hands me a spoon. "I didn't let you and Kareem down last year when you were co-captains. I won't start any of that this year now that we're seniors. I'm a good little college boy."

"Tell that to the puke bucket Sly got for you."

I nearly snort out my cereal. "He watched me puke?" I say, mouth muffled over cereal. *Way to make a great first impression, Omar.*

"I guess," Ravi replies. "Hurry up. Kareem is swinging by to pick you up so you can get dressed for our lunch thing."

"Oh crap, I forgot!" I eat faster and see Landon

walk out of this room. He's in his boxers, looking down and dragging his feet. "Sup man?"

"Mm," he grunts, reaching behind me for a toaster pastry.

"You going with us to the lunch thing?"

"No, have fun," he mutters. Poor guy is still suffering from his first real heartbreak. *I've been there...*

"Alright, if you wanna hang out later, text me," I say.

"Yeah, okay," he replies. Then his door closes. I don't really want to be here when Landon cries, jerks off, or some combination of the two, so I finish my food quickly.

Getting my things, I notice a bottle of water on the side table again. I'm touched that Steven's brother, a complete stranger, took it upon himself to take care of me. I owe him a million favors, but right now, I need to get a move on or Kareem will ditch me.

An hour later, Kareem and I meet up with Ravi and Paul, my suitemate who's a sophomore on the soccer team. We walk into the KU Athletics Center, ready to get our party on. We were invited a week ago by Logan Micucci, the Facilities Manager, to celebrate the eighth birthday of his boyfriend's nephew. Or rather, his boyfriend, Wei Wong, who also works at our school, invited us. It may sound complicated, but us soccer boys are really tight with all of them. We taught Wei's nephew Galen how to play soccer last semester, and it was like we all got to be the cool older brothers the kid never had. In short, it was so much fun, and we're happy to be able to celebrate his birthday.

Also, college kids never pass up on the opportunity to eat free pizza and cupcakes—score!

After greeting Logan and Wei, Galen pulls us into a game of soccer and we kick the ball with some kiddos for a few minutes before the food arrives. I'm waiting for Steven and Sly to arrive, anxious to make a good second impression. No, he hasn't met sober me, so I wanna make a good redo of my *first* impression. Why I want to impress some junior I've never met before is beyond me—maybe because he took care of me?

In any case, mere minutes later, the O'Rourke brothers arrive. As they chat with Wei, I'm struck by how similar they look. Steven has dangling brown hair, and Sly has glasses on, but they may as well be identical.

Steven walks over to kiss Ravi, and Sly is standing alone, so now's my chance. *Okay, Omar, don't fuck this up.*

I casually walk over, and Sly recognizes me. "Hey!" I greet him. *Is my face warm?*

"Hey, you're awake."

"Yup." I awkwardly chuckle and scratch my arm. "You're Sly right?"

"Ah, you've stopped calling me Steven. That's an improvement." He's grinning and messing with me, but I'll take it.

"Yeah, well, drunk me has double vision." I shrug and force out another laugh. "You should know I lost my ID card."

"Ah."

"I swear I don't make a habit of sleeping on random campus benches."

"Hey, I don't judge. Maybe it was some kink I've never heard of. I don't know." He lifts up his hands and we both chuckle. His smile is precious and I'm not sure why, but I want to keep him happy.

"But seriously, thank you. You saved my ass last night, and if there's anything—"

"Omar, Omar!" I look down to see little Galen Wong walking up to us. "We need a goalie. Will you be our goalie?"

"Uhh..." I look at Sly, who's staring at me expectantly. "Sure buddy! Sly, do you wanna play with us?"

"That would make our teams odd again!" Galen says, pouting.

"It's okay." Sly chuckles. "I'm no athlete. I heard you soccer guys are good. I'm just gonna go sit over here and watch."

"Okay," I reply. Galen pulls me by the hand, but I crane my neck back around. "We'll continue this conversation later, yeah?"

"Later...Alligator." He shakes his head and winces at his own weird comment, and I laugh.

"Bet." I hope he knows I'm serious. I jog to the floor space where all the eight-year-olds and college kids are waiting for me. "Alright," I holler. "Whose team am I on?"

Several minutes later, the cake has been cut and we're all standing about, mingling. Some kids have gone back to playing, and most of the parents are all chatting with each other. I turn my head and notice Sly sitting alone, a piece of cake in his lap. He was watching the kids play ball before, but now he is staring up, wide-eyed, at the walls of the Athletics Center. It's a huge complex, and he's new, so I get why he might be overwhelmed.

This is my chance. *Alright, Omar, time to make some friends.*

I slide up close to him, and he doesn't seem to notice me. My friends and I do this all the time, crowding in each other's space at the dining hall or on buses to games. Hell, we've started to just bunch up next to Steven when he's hanging out with us, so Sly should be no different.

I scooch closer to him on the bench and wrap my arm around him in a side-hug. Before I can make some cheeky remark, I feel him jerk away and jump up. He's standing, visibly shaken, and his plate of cake has splattered all over his tight khakis and the floor. He turns to me, looking mortified, and everyone around us has stopped chatting to look right at him.

Shit. I did this. I tried to make a friend, and I fucked it up.

4: Sly

Fuck, I'm the worst.

I turn around to see that guy Omar sitting next to where I was, his arm still floating in place. He looks shocked but not as embarrassed as I am. I can't believe I've made a huge mess of myself, all because I can't handle one stupid little touch. His surprising arm on my shoulder triggered my friggin' haphephobia, and now everyone's staring at me. *Way to make a good first impression at a big university, Sly.*

I slowly step over the splattered cake, and a tall man walks over to me. "Hey, you're making a mess of my Athletics Center. I'm the Facilities Manager, you know, and this building is my baby."

I want *to die.* I want to spontaneously combust and not let all of these people know I'm a freak who can't stand human contact. "I...am *so* sorry," I mutter through my gritted teeth.

The man—whom Steven introduced to me earlier as Logan —breaks out in a laugh. "Ahh, I'm just messin' with you, kid! It's what we do here. Right Omar?" I turn to see Omar, still looking shocked, but nodding now. "There's a restroom right over there. Go ahead and clean yourself up."

16

"But the floor…" I look down at all the cake bits below me.

"Don't worry about it! Go get yourself cleaned up, Mr. O'Rourke."

"Okay," I hang my head in shame and stiffly run to the bathroom.

Once inside, alone and safe, I splash some water on my lap. Great, now the chocolate has mixed with water, and it looks like all sorts of awful things have happened to my crotch.

Before I can dwell on my sad state, I feel something touch my shoulder and jump again. Omar's in the bathroom, and his eyebrows are up so high they may fly off his face at any moment.

"Fuck!" I huff.

"I'm sorry! I uhh…brought napkins." He holds a wad of brown papers to me. I hesitate, then quickly snatch them.

I close my eyes and try to catch my breath. This Omar guy is the reason I embarrassed myself in front of everyone. He keeps making me jolt, even after all I did for him last night.

"I'm really sorry, Sly. Now I owe you a million-and-one favors. If there's anything I can do for you, just name it."

I turn to the sink, irritated. I wet the napkins, then wipe my pants—it's actually working, sort of. "You really wanna help me?"

"Yes, anything."

I turn and look at him. "Stop embarrassing me, and please, leave me alone." I don't give him the chance to respond before I walk away, tossing out the wad of trash on the way out the door.

* * *

"You sure you don't want to go back to our apartment and change?" Steven asks while driving. "It'll take like five minutes."

"No, we're already out. Let's go buy groceries." I'm staring out the window on the passenger's side. I don't even care that my lap still has some brown stains and we're going out in public. I just needed to get out of that Athletics Center. I thought the low-key family party my brother dragged me to would be a fine social event for me to make friends and not embarrass myself, but I was wrong.

"Alright. We can stop by some clothing store and buy pants?"

"No, I'm fine," I reply brusquely. I know my brother is only trying to help, so it isn't fair of me to take my frustrations out on him.

"Look, Sly, we all have had our share of embarrassing situations. It's no big deal. The guys on the team won't even remember this by tomorrow."

"That's easy for you to say. They *have* to love you because Ravi loves you."

I look over to see Steven grinning. "Well, we're all roommates now. You'll get along with them soon enough, I'm sure." He pats my knee.

My immediate family are some of the only people I don't mind touching me. Heaven knows Steven and I used to have slap fights and wrestling matches as kids, so his patting me on the knee doesn't have the same effect as Omar's hand around me.

I reflect on how I blew up at him in the bathroom today. Shit, that was uncalled for. I'm so anxious after an embarrassing touch-related incident, but I still should not have said that to him. I need to apologize, but frankly, I'm still not in the right headspace.

"Besides," Steven continues, "since we're brothers, that makes Ravi like your brother-in-law. Since him, Omar, Kareem, and Landon are basically brothers... that's the transitive property, bro."

"I don't think that's how transitive property works," I reply, raising one eyebrow.

"Sure it is. You're brothers with the whole soccer team now too. They're family, like it or not."

"I suppose."

Steven takes an exit off the freeway. "They'll look out for you, and they'll even help wingman you to find you a girlfriend if you want. Korham is a great place for you to finally let loose a little."

"Whatever you say." I know he means well, but I don't like the idea of the entire men's soccer team looking after me like I'm some lost kitten. I need to make my own way at KU, not just be known as Steven's twin-but-a-year-younger brother. I need to let loose on my terms, find out who I really am, and work on my fear of physical intimacy.

5: Omar

After the birthday party, Kareem, Paul, and I make the trek back up to our dorm. Once inside, Vince, our other roommate, points at the table while playing video games. "Odom, this came for you."

I look down and see my ID card. "Sweet, thanks."

"Yeah, some girl came by," Vince continues, still not making eye contact. He jams the buttons on his controller and stares at the TV. "She seemed bummed not to be able to see you."

"Yeah, well...Girls be trippin' and all that." I shrug and unlock my door. Before I can go in and shut it, Kareem stops in the doorway.

"Are you alright, man?"

"Yeah." I nod my head, then look up and plaster on a big fake smile. "Why wouldn't I be?"

"Well, Steven's brother made a mess. I wasn't sure if you felt guilty or not."

I try not to let my smile slip. That is, indeed, part

of why I'm not feeling so hot. "It's all good, man. No harm done, right? Listen, we getting dining hall dinner tonight?"

Kareem stares at me dubiously for a bit, then looks away. "I'm having dinner with Stacia. What about tomorrow before practice?"

"Can't. I have my independent study most of the afternoon." I sit down at my desk and boot up my PC.

"That sucks. It's our last semester and..." His voice trails off and he looks down.

"Maybe after?" I ask, and a hopeful look shines on his face. "So, you two survived the big summer break, huh?"

He rolls his eyes. "Yeah, yeah..."

"Kareem Hall with the same girl two semesters in a row. I never thought I'd live to see the day."

"Well..." He taps on my door frame and looks up. "Random hook-ups don't hold the same appeal anymore, ya know? We're seniors, not freshmen."

I nod and look down. I want to throw back a witty retort, but I can't. It's true that no-strings-attached has been my MO thus far, but Kareem and Ravi both settling down has me reconsidering things.

"Ehh, who am I kidding?" Kareem is grinning and says, "I'm talking to the king of breaking the hearts of all the girls and guys at KU."

"Damn straight. Err...sometimes straight. And don't you forget it." I go back to my signature cocky smile, and Kareem chuckles.

"Later, man." He leaves, closing my door, and I'm left alone with my thoughts. I dwell on the look of disdain on Sly's face from earlier. I really screwed him over, and now he wants me to stay away. That sucks 'cause he's kinda cute...

21

Nope. Not going down that train of thought. He's Ravi's boyfriend's brother, so he is off-limits. It's in the soccer bro code. I think.

Instead, I boot up my class schedule online to find out who I'm doing my independent study credit with to finish my English degree. Hopefully the theater professor is chill and low-key.

"Theater…" the woman announces, walking across the stage. She opens her arms and continues to monologue, "…is the very *lifeblood* of humanity as a whole! Drama is the backbone of the arts world, and it supports the musculature of music, dance, visual arts, and literature!" She spins, then flips her brown hair, staring right at me. "Wouldn't you agree?"

Her voice echoes through the auditorium, and I look around. I'm sitting in the audience alone. "Oh um, are you asking me? Uh…yes?" I flinch at my timid answer.

"So, you're my independent study ward this semester?" She hops off the stage and saunters toward me. "You shall be my assistant as we put together Korham University's fall stage show. I'm your director. Pleasure to meet you…"

"It's Omar, Professor Hark." I smile. She definitely has the theatrics down.

"Rule number one, please call me Aggie whenever possible. It keeps me young. Walk with me." She strides quickly toward the stairs on the right, and I try to keep up. "Now you're going to learn the ins and outs of the theater and help me run our adaptation of *Izumi and Alex*. By November, you'll know everything about how the stage works and have learned the script by heart."

We walk up to the stage, and she spins on her heels, so I'm forced to stop. "If these curtains could talk, do you know what they'd say?" She pauses and I stare at her. I hope she's not expecting an answer from me.

"They'd say, '*OMAR!*'" I jump at her shrill outburst. "Bring our show...to *life!*" She throws her hands up in the air, beaming at me, and I nearly applaud at her spectacle. Aggie is over the top, but I'm digging her zest and attitude. It feels like I'm in a movie of my own simply being around her.

I smile at her, but before I can get a word in edgewise, she continues her speech. "There's a lot to go over, but I already have many sign-ups for tomorrow evening's auditions." She walks and I follow her, wishing I had a paper to take notes on. "I need you by my side constantly during the production process. You're gonna be my second pair of eyes, ears, and hands, making sure that the show, *indeed*, goes on as scheduled."

She pauses and turns to me. "Are you a fan of romantic shows and movies?"

A broad grin grows on my face. "Hell yeah."

She smiles. "Great. I expect excellence from you, Mr. Odom, and if you put in the effort, you'll for sure get an A. Now follow me while I show you the backstage area."

She keeps walking, and I try to keep up, but now I'm hyped. *Izumi and Alex* isn't a very common play, but it's so romantic. I can already see it being a work of art. Auditions are tomorrow, and I'm psyched to be a part of it all. There's something hopeful about this independent study course that grows in my belly, but I don't know what it is. No matter what, this sounds like an awesome way to spend my final fall semester at Korham University.

6: Sly

"And how are you adjusting to living in an apartment together?" Steven and I stare at our mother's face in the smart phone. She insisted on video-chatting us tonight, so we chose to share screen time with her for one conversation—college is all about time management. "Do you have enough money for food?"

"Yes, Mom," we say in unison. We turn to look at each other, taken aback by our synchronous voices.

"Oh good. I'm so proud of you, boys. Your nieces miss you."

"You'll see us soon enough," Steven replies.

"Holidays and such," I add, nodding.

"I know. Soon, Steven, you'll be all graduated, and Sly, you'll be right after." We can hear her voice start to waver.

"Mom..." We both groan, smiling and rolling our eyes. We were trying to avoid this weird display of emotion. Our mom is great, but we don't want to listen to her get all teary-eyed over the phone.

"It's within my right as a mother to be proud of my boys! I love you both. Your father and sister love you, too. We want you to succeed."

"We love you too," Steven says while I once again nod.

"Good. Now Steven, is Sly making friends?"

"Mom! I'm right here!" I glare at the phone camera indignantly.

"I know, but your older brother should be looking out for you." Her tone is scolding, but I'm not sure whom she's chastising.

"I'm sure Sly is making friends," Steven says. I don't miss him side-eye glancing at me for a brief moment. "Today was only the first day of classes. Soon, he'll be partying it up like the rest of us."

I want to defend myself, but my brother is clearly saying whatever it takes to get our mom off my back.

"Well, I hope you don't do too much partying," Mom continues.

"I won't. Not when I'm busy with my sociology degree." I look up and see Landon rush into his room, Ravi trailing not far behind him. "It's not like I'm dating the captain of the soccer team. Speaking of..." I wave my hand to beckon Ravi to come join us.

He walks over with a smile and crowds next to Steven. "Who's that?" Mom asks.

"Hi Mrs. O'Rourke," Ravi greets her with a polite smile. His arm is around my brother's shoulder. I scooch over, already feeling like a third wheel.

"Oh Ravi! Look at you! How are you sweetie?"

"I'm great." He and Steven both chuckle and entertain my mom for the next five minutes until we bid our farewells.

As I walk to my room in the apartment, I hear Steven say, "Hey, Sly."

I turn around, and Ravi is on his lap on the couch. Ew. I'm happy for them considering all the drama that unfolded last year, but I don't need to see my brother being all lovey-dovey on our shared furniture. He gets to be the carefree, popular brother who enjoys physical contact; I don't need to be more jealous of him and his capacity to have a relationship. "Ravi and I were going to go get food. Want to come?"

"Um, no thanks," I reply, looking down at the carpet. "I have a lot of...reading to do."

"Already? We had one day of classes."

"Yeah," I mutter, quickly closing the door.

I boot up my PC and start scouring the web to find a video to prepare myself for tomorrow. I'm at a big-name university now with a fancy Fine Arts building, including an entire theater department. I search for various productions of *Izumi and Alex*, a musical known for being crazy romantic. I was excited to find out it is this year's semester show.

I refuse to be that fly-on-the-wall, shy guy anymore—that was the old Sly. I'm here at KU to broaden my horizons. This year, I want to be a part of a real college stage production. I've always loved romance in all mediums, and this musical is the perfect place for me to grow.

I'm aware this show requires kissing scenes in front of an audience. The idea makes nervous as hell, but that's the point. I want to push myself out of my comfort zone so I can grow into the guy I want to be. If I get the role, with enough practice I just might get used to physical touch! On top of that, I won't be seen as that awkward, shy guy anymore—I'll be a performing artist in the theater!

If I play the guy who gets the girl in a musical, maybe it will bleed over into real life; I will finally be able to become the extroverted Sly I've always wanted to be and find a romance of my own.

I'm not feeling so hot about my master plan anymore. It's the day of the auditions, and I'm sitting in the auditorium with at least thirty other students. Everyone's reading the small scripts we were handed when we came in. I'm trying to focus on the lines like everyone else, but I can't help looking up at the stage and shaking my knee.

Aggie, the director, is the loudest, most dramatic woman I've ever seen, and she only talked for like five minutes. That's fine, whatever, she's the drama teacher and she's faculty, so that's her prerogative. But to her left—stage left? I'm not sure—is none other than her assistant director... Omar.

I thought jocks never came to the Fine Arts building! What gives?

"Fate is truly a fickle, unforgiving mistress," some guy says in the seat behind me. He's reading the script, but I can't help agreeing. What are the odds the guy who embarrassed me the other day is now second-in-command for this extracurricular activity? Just my luck—what's he gonna do, somehow make my voice crack when I sing on stage for the first time?

I take a deep breath and force my knee to stop bouncing. I remind myself Omar never meant to hurt me; the cake thing was an accident. Ravi and Steven say only good things about him. I overreacted when I told him to leave me alone because I had a haphephobic incident. Even if he wasn't in charge of my audition, I need to apologize to Omar.

Man, doing the mature thing sucks.

I look back down at the script and try to reread some lines while I wait for my turn. Twenty minutes pass while other students get up, reading for the roles of the titular Izumi or Alex. Every time I glance up, Omar and Aggie are deep in conversation. Earlier, the professor gave me a number on a paper as my identity for the audition and I doubt Omar has even noticed me sitting here since.

Reading the lines over some more, I finally hear my number called out. "105!" Omar shouts, looking down at his clipboard and walking across the stage. I stand up and try to will my legs to stop trembling. I make it up the stage stairs and stand in front of the two while holding my numbered paper up to my chest.

"Name?" Omar asks, still not looking at me.

"Sylvester."

"Sylvester..." Omar repeats, while he and Aggie look down at their papers.

"Sylvester O'Rourke. But you can call me Sly."

Omar's eyes snap up and recognition flies across his face like a shooting star. His jaw drops, but I smirk at him. "I'm here to audition for the role of Alex."

7: Omar

I gape at Sly and try to form words; he is the last person I expected at the audition.

"I remember you from Logan's party," Aggie says. "Okay, so what brings you here, Mr. O'Rourke?"

"Like I said," he begins. "I'm here for the role of Alex." His grin is challenging and directed toward me. He's taken off his glasses and seems so confident on stage, channeling his brother. But unlike Steven, Sly is really piercing me with his stare, as if to say, *I belong here. You gonna do something about it?*

I have to admit I find his self-assured demeanor really sexy.

"Mm…Alex is more of an arrogant character," Aggie remarks, tapping her chin. "Would you be interested in auditioning for another role at my suggestion?" Aggie grins, and I turn back to see Sly's smile falter.

"Um…who did you have in mind?"

"Dakin, the ethereal trickster." Sly seems taken aback by her words, and I'm inclined to agree.

"Isn't Dakin a girl?"

"No one's gender is set in stone in this show." Aggie shrugs and leans back, her arm draping over the chair. "It's the 21st century, Mr. O'Rourke. And Dakin and Ezekiel are just as important as Izumi and Alex."

"I um…" Sly looks perplexed and defeated. His grip on the script hardens as he looks left and right. "I've been looking over Alex's lines."

"That's fine!" Aggie smiles at him then turns to me. "Omar, you know this play, right?"

"Inside and out, ma'am…I mean, Aggie."

"Then tell Mr. O'Rourke all about Dakin."

I gulp audibly and look down at my scripts. "Well…Dakin floats around, boasting that her, I mean, *his* magic is the most powerful in all the kingdom. In act one, anyway." I look up and see Sly staring at me intently. This time, there's no sign of a challenge, but a softening of his eyes. He's really listening to me.

"In act two, he realizes he actually enjoys the company of Prince Ezekiel. They have that awesome song, and…well, they find their true love. There's so much growth in Dakin's character throughout the show, and that's what makes him one of the most fascinating characters. I'd argue he's just as memorable as Lady Macbeth or Juliet."

There's a spark of understanding that bounces across Sly's eyes. When I'm done talking, I realize the entire auditorium is listening to me.

"Well, that was wonderful!" Aggie pats me on the shoulder. "I couldn't have said it better myself! So what do you say, Mr. O'Rourke? I'd like you to audition for Dakin, but it's up to you."

After a long moment, Sly shrugs. "I don't know

the lines that well, but I'd be willing to look them over and
—"

"Perfect! Omar, give him the other script, and
you can run lines now!"

I hesitate, then get up, exchanging scripts with
Sly, trying not to make eye contact. All I've done is mess with
this guy since he got to KU, and, while this isn't my fault, I
still feel guilty.

Sly leafs through the words then clears his
throat. "So uh...I start on scene three?"

"Perfect. It's okay if you didn't memorize it."
Aggie turns to me. "Omar will read the other character."

I nod as Sly shakes out his shoulders. He stares
at the script then starts to read out loud as Dakin. "What is
an esteemed knight as yourself doing wandering in a
forgotten swamp such as this?"

He sounds so flirty that my cheeks get warm. A
part of me wishes he was actually directing that charm at
me. *They're just lines, Omar. Keep it professional.* "My fair maiden
—or uh, gentlesir. I do not wander. I seek the golden rattle of
the lost princess," I reply, in character, as Ezekiel.

"Well, such treasures are only folklore. They
cannot be unearthed by those unwilling"—he looks down
and reads more lines, then continues— "to open their hearts
and minds. Are you..." Sly looks down again, then back up
with a gorgeous grin. "A believer of the legends?"

I look down at my lines. "The only concept I do
not believe in is disbelief. My imagination..." I stare at Sly,
then manage to crack a half-grin. "...is unhinged. I have faith.
And beautiful gentlesirs such as yourself only strengthen my
resolve." I glance at the lines again. "Will you be joining me
on such a quest?"

Sly looks back up from his script. "You will not find what you seek here in this barren swamp!"

"The scene changes from dark to a lush green," Aggie announces, also reading the script. "Dakin is using her, uh, *his* magic to alter the scene."

Sly waves his arms around like an inflatable toy, and the auditorium hums with laughter. He's pretending to use magic like Dakin. The fact that he's already getting into character is both amusing and attractive. "For it is now a vibrant forest! Your eyes are playing tricks on you. It was never a swamp. Perhaps you need some rest, my esteemed knight."

I read over my script quickly and catch Sly's eyes with my gaze. "Call me Ezekiel." I grin, and for a moment, Sly's smile flattens before he regains his composure. "I must know your name, fair gentlesir. I must know everything about you. I wish for your company."

I don't even know who's saying the words now, Ezekiel or Omar.

"You...have not yet earned my name," Sly says, not breaking eye contact.

A silent moment passes between us before Aggie starts clapping. "Alright, I think I've seen enough. Thank you!" There's a small smattering of applause, and Sly walks off stage. "Alright next up is...what number is next Omar?"

I wake up from my daze. That's right; independent study credits, that's why I'm here. "Next up is number 106!" I holler.

After auditions, I catch up to Sly right outside

33

the Fine Arts building. He's walking slowly, but my soccer stride makes it easy to round on him. "Hey!"

"Hey." He offers me a small smile but doesn't stop walking.

"That was um...good job in there!"

"Thanks. Should you be telling me that? I auditioned, and you're the assistant director."

"Aggie makes most of the decisions, so..." My voice trails off and I shrug. The sun is almost setting on this warm late summer day, and none of the people scattered about the quad pay us any mind. "I wanted to tell you...I didn't know you were auditioning."

"Well, I randomly signed up a couple of days ago, so that checks out."

"Right. Sorry I keep bumping into you. I swear I didn't know she was going to change the role you were auditioning for."

"No worries." He's still walking. He's giving me a not-quite-cold shoulder—more like a room-temperature shoulder.

"And I'm sorry if working with me on the play is going to be...weird."

"Why would it be weird?"

"Because you told me to fuck off the other day?" At this, Sly finally stops.

"Look...that was an overreaction." He stares at me and the sunset catches his face in a perfect way, the orange bouncing off his smooth skin. "I'm sorry. I just have this thing about being touched. It's not just you."

"Oh." That explains a lot. I look down and process it, then smile at him again. "I won't be doing that anymore, I promise." I put my hands up like I'm being robbed and take a step back. This earns me a genuine smile from him and we keep walking. "You really owned the role today."

"Thanks. Could you do me a favor? Could you not tell my brother or Ravi that I'm auditioning? I don't want to get anyone's expectations up and not make the cut."

"No doubt, man. My lips...sealed." I motion like I'm zipping my mouth and he almost chuckles. We walk in an easy silence for another minute or so, making it back to where the jock dorms are.

"Well, this is me," I say.

"Cool. I'm headed to the library for a little bit."

"Reading some books?"

"Ah, so you've been there," he quips, lips hitching up into a grin.

"Hey, I'm an English major! Plus, I love their romantic fiction section."

"Really?" He smiles and pushes up his glasses.

"Yeah, I check out romance novels. Total nerd here. Go ahead. You can poke fun at me." I grin and he shakes his head.

"I would never. That's what I read, too."

"Oh cool." Sly likes romance novels, too? That makes my heart buzz a little, but I'm not sure why. "We should exchange book recommendations some time."

"As long as you don't tell my brother. He wouldn't get it."

"Dude!" I laugh. "The soccer team would absolutely roast me if they knew how much romance I read." We both laugh.

"Then I guess it's our common secret."

Our laughter dies down, and I take in how calm and

handsome he looks right now. "Cool," I finally say. "Well, goodnight. And good luck with getting the part. Even if you don't, I hope you consider joining stage crew. I need some strong hands on my team."

"Careful, Omar." He walks backward. "If I didn't know any better, I'd think you want me around to take orders from you." My face turns warm and my throat goes dry. I think he winks, but in the near-darkness of sunset, it's hard to tell. I'm so used to flirting with anyone; you'd think I could take some innuendo without choking up. "Later, man," he hollers. He spins around on his heels then strides away.

I'm left standing there watching him walk to the library. I can't get past how attracted I was to Sly on stage and the witty banter we had just now. Nope. *Tamp those feelings down, Omar.* Ravi's boyfriend's little brother is like my brother, so he's off-limits, no matter how cute he is.

8: Sly

I awkwardly nod my head along to the music and sip on a juice box while the students around me mingle. Today I'm at the Queer Pride Union office, which is located above the KU Student Union. It's a large loft with a desk, a sound system, chairs, and tables, all littered with safe sex paraphernalia. On this occasion, however, they've placed snacks and games everywhere as part of their back-to-school casual meeting. I recognize a couple of my brother's friends, but there are at least twenty people here I've never seen before, all ignoring me.

That's fine by me; I only let Steven and Ravi drag me here because I need to get my mind off the auditions. It's nerve-racking, putting yourself out there, but I have to wait for Aggie to make her decision. She seemed pretty keen on the idea of me playing a gender-swapped version of Dakin the fairy, but I would find out in a matter of days.

A girl with light-brown skin and red-framed glasses walks up to me. "Hey!" she greets me and I'm forced to take my mouth off the straw.

"Uh, hi."

"I'm Steven's main girl." She shrugs and smiles at me. I recognize her from social media pictures. "You must be Sly."

"Guilty." I shrug and offer a shy smile. "And you are..."

"Simone. Thanks for coming to this meeting. We welcome all orientations here at Korham U."

"Well, Steven's the gay one." I look down, then pull my eyes back up. "Not that there's anything wrong with that!" I add quickly.

"It's cool," Simone chuckles. "And it's not only gays. The queer community has so many labels and sublabels." She stands next to me, and it forces me to look out into the crowd. While I had read all about the LGBTQ+ community, there weren't that many out-and-proud folks at my community college. I really am broadening my horizons by coming to this university. "I want to stress that we're accepting of everyone."

"Well, I guess I'm just an ally." I've never really considered myself as part of the queer community. I'm not like Steven, Ravi, or even Omar—the idea of being intimate with anyone at all makes me squirm.

"It's cool." We're both quiet for a moment, letting the music and chatter surround us. "These meetings are fun, but we strive to help the queer community as a whole."

"How so?" Helping people is my jam. Plus, getting Simone to talk puts the heat off me.

"We hold charity events. We put up flyers to raise awareness. And we also have Safe Space office hours."

"What's that?"

"It's a confidential place for anyone who wants to talk about their identity issues." I look up and see Simone studying me. I can tell she wants to say something, but she wants me to read between the lines first. "The next one is here tomorrow after six."

"I uh..." I scratch my neck and look down. Her gaze is making me uncomfortable, like she's seeing truths I would rather keep under the rug. "I think I'm straight. I mean, good." My eyes quickly jump back to hers, and I shake my head. "Not that I equate being straight to being inherently good, because I don't!"

Simone once again giggles. "Don't sweat it, Sly!" She goes to put her hand on my shoulder, and I instinctively scoot away. Her face falls for a second, but then she's smiling again. "I wanted to let you know...if you ever need to get anything off your chest, we're here for you."

"You run Safe Space?"

"It's mostly the QPU e-board, along with the faculty advisor, who couldn't make it tonight. I'm helping this semester because the vice president is away on sabbatical. He's out dancing in New York City. My dumb ass decided to volunteer to fill in because I live in a house with most of the e-board."

"Ah, I take it you don't want to deal with this?" I take a sip and she looks down.

"At first I didn't, but now, I've grown to like it." She nods and looks up. "I feel like I'm giving back and helping people in need."

"That's very admirable."

She smiles then, it fades as she looks left and right. No one is close enough to eavesdrop, so she lowers her voice. "Look, Sly, not everyone's coming out story is cut-and-dry."

My eyebrows furrow. "What makes you think I

need to come out?"

"I don't. I was just thinking about how tense Ravi was before he started dating Steven openly. He had the *biggest* crush on your brother, but Steven wasn't so sure of Ravi's intentions." We look over to where Ravi and Steven are playing a video game of virtual tennis. They're laughing, and as usual, no one can put a smile on my brother's face like Ravi can. "QPU strives to be a place where everyone can be comfortable in their own skin."

She turns to me, and once again there's a weighted silence. Is it *that* obvious I have some issues when it comes to having sex or wanting a romantic partner? I feel like I'm starting to sweat, and the room is getting warmer.

"Come on," she says, pushing off the table she was leaning on. "They're finally done, and I wanna play virtual bowling. Think you can take me, *Little O'Rourke*?" Her eyebrows wag in playful challenge.

"Bring it on...Whatever-your-last-name-is." She cackles, and we walk over to Steven and Ravi to ask for a turn at the game.

When we get back to the apartment, Landon is in the living room in just his boxers, watching TV, wearing his signature frown. The poor guy is hurting, but Steven told me not to ask any questions. Next to him on the couch, Omar is happily munching on popcorn.

"Oh, hey guys!" Omar greets us with a smile, and a kernel of popcorn falls out of his mouth.

"Sup man," Ravi says, plopping down next to Landon. Steven nods and goes into the room he and Ravi share.

Omar makes hopeful eye contact with me. "We're watching *The Forever Squadron* movie. Want to join us, Sly?"

"No thanks, I um...should go study." I swear Omar looks disappointed, but I'm not sure why.

"Didn't we watch this last semester?" Ravi asks as I unlock my door.

"Yeah, but I wasn't paying attention *at all* that night," Landon replies.

Once I'm sequestered in the safety of my room, I boot up my PC. I look over some emails from professors, but what I'm really looking for is the audition results. I need to know if I made the callback—the suspense is killing me!

There's a soft knock on my door. I holler, "Come in!" without bothering to look up.

"Hey." I glance up to see Omar standing there. He shuts the door behind him quietly, and it suddenly feels like my single room is the size of a church confessional.

"Omar..." I take my glasses off and look right at him. He's got on a black t-shirt and tight blue jeans. A day's growth is on his cheeks, and his brown stubble is really coming in. With that smile on his face, he looks quite attractive—if you're into jocks with toned bodies, trimmed hair, and mocha complexion. "Uh, what...what's up?"

"Landon went to the bathroom and Ravi and Steven are probably hooking up or something," he says in a hushed tone. "But I wanted to talk to you."

"What about?" I ask. My heart is starting to speed up.

"Sly, you got the part of Dakin," he whispers.

"Really?" I jump out of my seat, and Omar laughs.

41

"Yes! Well, you're going to get a follow-up email tomorrow from yours truly." He shrugs and smiles. He's cocky, but I would be too if I was a handsome, popular jock. "And you need to do a callback where you sing a prepared piece. I'm going to email you the list of songs to practice. It's really simple."

"Oh...okay...I can do that." I look down and bite my lip. I don't exactly have vocal training, but I knew I'd have to sing if I got the part.

"But yeah, Aggie was *totally* impressed by your audition. You're basically a shoo-in!" Omar's eyes twinkle with excitement.

"That's amazing!" I say, nearly shouting. He puts his finger to his lip and I hunch my shoulders. "Wait, why am I whispering?" I ask, my voice much lower.

"Because I'm not supposed to tell people until tomorrow."

"Then, why are you telling me today?"

"I wanted to share the good news with you. You're one of us now; you're a KU soccer boy."

I look at him incredulously. "Soccer? Me?"

"Look, the co-captain is dating your brother." Omar grins. "That effectively makes you and me brothers. It's called transitive property."

"You're not the first person to tell me that." I awkwardly chuckle and scratch my arm. "Thank you."

We smile at each other and something strange passes between us. It's silent, but it's like I can feel something unseen growing here? What is this momentary warmth that's coursing through my veins?

"I guess I'll see you at rehearsal. Goodnight." Omar leaves and quietly shuts the door and I'm left standing there stunned.

I came to KU to expand my horizons—well, getting this part will certainly do that. But everything's shifting between me and Steven's friends, and I don't know if it's good or bad. All I know is I have a lot of questions I need to ask myself and some singing to practice.

9: Omar

I walk to my cubby in the locker room while I towel off. It's only the second practice of the season, but Coach Dacks is running us ragged. The end-of-summer heat in New York isn't helping the sweaty situation, but it's all worth it to get to play the game I love. Hanging out with my bros and getting attention from all the ladies and some dudes? Being on the soccer team is the life! It sucks this is our final year, so I have to make the most of it.

"We going out tonight?" Kareem asks while I put on my pants.

"Oof, rain check. I have to do all sorts of crap for my independent study," I reply. "What about Saturday?"

"I'm going to Stacia's family reunion thing."

"*Ooh*," I coo as I pull my shirt on. "Getting serious." I wag my eyebrows and Ravi smiles at us nearby.

"We've been dating for almost a year," Kareem replies. "Ravi?"

"Sorry, I'm busy going to an art thing with Steven," Ravi adds.

"An 'art thing'? Is that what the kids are calling it now?" I ask, my voice dripping with innuendo.

Ravi chuckles and shakes his head. Landon walks up to us, looking slightly less depressed than usual. "You sure you can't hang out tonight, Omar?"

"No, sorry I..." My voice trails off after I turn on my phone and see the notification; my dad called. Great, just what I need. "I gotta take this, guys. Later."

"Peace," Ravi says as I walk out of the room.

I find a secluded hallway and dial my dad's number. He should know I shut off my phone during practice, but I'd be surprised if he remembers I'm on a sports team at all.

After two rings, I hear his voice. "Omar."

"Hi Dad." I clear my throat and close my eyes. "What uh...what's up?"

"I'm simply checking up on you. Your mother and I haven't heard from you since you drove to school."

"Yeah, well, I had practice. You know...soccer practice."

"Enough about that," he interjects. "How are your classes?"

"Classes are...fine." I look up at the ceiling and stare at the stray marks on the tiles. I'll focus on anything other than this conversation right now.

"You're a prelaw major or a premed major?"

"I told you, I'm an English major," I reply, trying not to groan.

"Don't say 'I told you,' Omar. It's not polite. You need to make sure you're getting *our* money's worth of an education."

"Yes, Dad," I say through gritted teeth.

"What is your plan for after graduation?"

"I uh..." I close my eyes and put my left hand on my forehead. "I don't know yet."

"Well, when we let you pick English as your major we assumed you'd have a plan for after college."

"You *let* me pick English?"

"You didn't want to do premed, that's fine," he continues, ignoring my dubious remark. "But I'd like to know the plan for next fall." I try not to groan. Of the many things I'm in denial about, my career after college might be the biggest one. Meanwhile, my dad is *obsessed* with planning. I'm pretty sure he planned to have one son and one daughter because my sister and I are what he got. "You could probably still go to law school with your English degree."

"I don't know about that." The idea of being a lawyer doesn't interest me, but I don't say that. I just want this conversation to be over.

"Or you could even get your master's degree in education. Teach English to other college kids?" The idea of being an English teacher is intriguing. But then again, it gives me icky flashbacks of high school literature class and *her*...

"Um maybe...Look I gotta go. I actually have a lot of homework to do."

"Okay, I'll let you go. But I need you to know one thing, Omar."

"And what's that?" I ask through more gritted teeth.

"Your mother and I won't be around forever to fund your academics. You need to be able to make money and a name for yourself. You're not that nineteen-year-old we sent off to Korham anymore. You're a twenty-three-year-old man. Your future is now on you."

"Yes, Dad."

"Okay. Your mother, sister, and I pray for your success. Goodnight."

"Night, Dad." The phone beeps, and I finally take in a deep breath. I look out at the darkness through the window and lean my forehead on the glass.

As annoyed as I am, I know he's right. I need a sense of purpose, but the only thing I really ever cared about was reading and writing, specifically rom-com screenplays. Frankly, not only do I doubt I'm good enough to make that a career, but it brings back such sour memories from high school.

I straighten my back and take another deep breath. I smile at my reflection, then turn to walk away. I'm not going to think depressing thoughts. Those can just go into a shoebox labeled 'Omar's denials,' shoved underneath the bed of my subconscious. I have papers to write, class reading to do, and a cast list to update for the show I'm partially responsible for.

"On behalf of myself and Omar, we want to congratulate you all on making the cast!" Everyone claps while Aggie beams at us from the center table. I'm seated next to her, and there are two other rectangular tables jutting out on either side of us. A few days ago, Aggie finished the musical callback auditions. Afterward, I sent out the official emails letting everyone know who got cast.

Today there are about fifteen people in this room, including Sly O'Rourke—he's sitting to my left, staring intently at the script. He removes his glasses and squints, making him look like a cute elderly man. "Now I'll let my assistant director here hand out the contracts. We at Korham University take the dramatic arts *very* seriously."

I get up and walk to the end of one table, handing each cast member a sheet. "I'll need you all to sign these and give them to me by Friday!" Aggie announces over the murmurs of the cast. "If you can't make the rehearsal dates or the actual show, it might be best for you to drop out so we can cast someone else. We want you all to be here, but I understand you might have other commitments."

I pause and look up. It hadn't even occurred to me that soccer might get in the way of this production I'm a part of. If we do well this season, I am going to be on the road to a lot of games. I have a soccer scholarship, so I'll need to be there. Still, this is for my grade, and I don't want to miss any shows. *Shit.*

"Omar?" I'm broken out of my daze by Sly, who has turned around in his chair. He's got a concerned look on his face as he stares at me.

"Hm?"

"The contracts? In your hand?" He's pointing at my stack of papers; I froze before giving them out to the cast. *Whoops.*

I shake my head then grin. "My bad, O'Rourke. Here ya go." He takes one and continues to stare at me. I just nod and keep walking, not wanting him to realize anything's wrong. I give out the rest of the contracts, then take my seat.

"Now, I'll give you all time to go over the dates and the contract," Aggie says. She puts her glasses down and opens up her script. "But in the meantime, I want us to get started on building cast chemistry. Let's all go around and introduce ourselves and what roles we're going to be playing this semester."

Starting from the right, folks take turns saying their names and who's playing whom. When it's Sly's turn, he gets up and gives a shy wave to everyone.

"Hi. I'm Sly. I'm playing the role of Dakin. In this version, he's a guy, though, so Aggie says I won't be in drag. What a shame." Everyone laughs, and he gives a confident smile. I'm proud of him for being so outspoken and charming. It's adorable—in a platonic way, of course. He's my best friend's boyfriend's brother, and he's in this play. I can't have the hots for him. *Bad Omar, suppress those feelings.*

The very last person to introduce themselves is a tall, thin guy with brown hair and a beard. He looks gangly, but he stands with confidence and an easy smile. At the audition, his voice was loud and clear, and he really owned his role. "Hey, everyone," the guy says. "I'm Charles. I'll be playing 'Ezekiel,' the love interest of the fairy Dakin. I mean, the uh, male fairy Dakin."

"Yes, Mr. Rodon, can you sit over here?" Aggie beckons him over. "I want you to start building chemistry with Mr. O'Rourke." She taps me on the shoulder and I turn to her. "Omar, dear, switch seats with him."

"Uhh..." I turn back to my left to see Charles towering behind Sly, who's looking at him as well.

"We need the cast to bond, and this makes the most sense. I want to build an authentic romance." Aggie looks back down at her script while she makes a sweeping motion with her left hand, telling me to leave.

As I walk away with all my papers, I turn back

around to see Sly opening up my chair for Charles. "Hey, I guess we're gonna be working together a lot," Charles says.

"Nice to meet you," Sly replies. I knew they were going to be playing love interests. So why do I have the sudden urge to break Charles's leg? Not in like the theater "good luck" sense—I literally want to break his leg, and I don't know why.

10: Sly

Things have been looking up the past two weeks at Korham University. I didn't butcher my singing audition and got a lead role in the fall musical. Classes are going well, and I've been making friends at play practice. There haven't been any more embarrassing cake-related incidents, and I've gotten the hang of finding my way around campus.

Today was going to be the next big step in my plan to broaden my horizons. I'm walking up the stairs of the Student Union building, and I'm nervous as hell. Steven's friend Simone told me about QPU Safe Space, but now that I'm actually walking up there, my palms are all sweaty. *What do I say to this person?* After some self-reflection the past few weeks, there's plenty I'd like to discuss, and QPU sounds like the place to be for me.

I'm two doors down when I see Simone herself walk out and close the door. I freeze, and her eyebrows jump when she looks at me. "Steven's brother!"

I roll my eyes. "It's Sly."

"Sorry. You're here for QPU?"

"Yeah, I want to see if um..." I look around and wipe my hands on my jeans.

"Got it. Say no more. We're all sworn to confidentiality."

"You're not the one running today's, um, thing?"

"No," she says. "I got a shift at my job at the library. But there's someone in there who is ready and willing to talk to you. Again, we're here to help, judgment-free zone."

I crack a small smile. Simone seems to really want me to feel welcome. "Alright then."

"Later, Steven's brother. I mean Sly." She dashes away, and I'm stuck with my sweaty palms alone in the hallway. After a moment, I steel myself, turn around and take two steps toward the closed door. *Moment of truth, Sly.*

Walking in, I instantly recognize the guy sitting at the desk, fiddling on his phone. He's Ravi and Steven's professor friend, the Asian guy who looks like he could be a supermodel. His eyes shine when he sees me. "Oh! Hello!"

"Hi um..." I clear my throat. "I'm here for..."

"For office hours?" I manage a slight nod while looking around the room. There's only the two of us in this massive loft, but the walls feel tight around me. My heart is pounding fast as I close and lock the door.

"Please have a seat!" I sit down and try to focus on the ambient buzzing sounds of the ventilation system. It's too quiet in here. I'm getting anxious. "I recognize you from my nephew's party!"

"Yup." I wince. "I'm the weirdo who made a mess on my lap."

"Did you? I don't recall..." His eyes dart down, pondering, then right back up at me. His dark eyes are warm and inviting; I can see why that Facilities Manager guy is dating him. "Anyway, my name is Wei. I'm the faculty advisor and for this hour I'm running QPU Safe Space office hours. Anything you say here will be held confidential, unless you're planning on hurting anyone."

"Okay." I nod and look down at my hands, tapping my thumbs together. There's so much I want to say, but the words won't come.

"Whenever you're ready, you can talk," Wei says. I nod, and another silent moment passes by while I stare at the tiles on the floor. "You're Steven's brother, right?"

I huff. "Yeah, that's what everyone calls me. It's like I don't even have a name anymore."

"Well, you never told me your name." I look up and see him smiling.

"Sorry...I'm Sylvester, but everyone calls me Sly."

"Sly, a pleasure to formally meet you. Would it help if I talked about myself?" I shrug. I don't see it being any worse than my silent treatment. "Truth is, I knew I was gay when I was sixteen."

"I'm not gay!" I blurt quickly.

"Alright, alright," Wei says, putting his hands up. "I don't mean to label you, just talking about myself here."

"Right, sorry," I mutter, looking back down. *I'm so stupid.*

"Not everyone's journey of self-discovery is the same. Mine just happened during puberty; I wasn't fantasizing about the girls in my class, but I felt drawn to the boys in my grade."

I laugh, looking up at the ceiling. "I can definitely relate to the first part of that."

"And the second part? About me starting to like men? Is that...something you've experienced or...not experienced?" I look directly at him. Wei seems to genuinely want me to open up. He's not judging me, and I feel like I can express myself.

"Well..." I look all around the room and wipe my hands on my lap. "I'm not...like Steven. Steven's had boyfriends. He clearly likes guys. His journey was rough at times, but my parents always accepted him. I didn't mind. Deep down, I've always been jealous of him."

"And can I ask why that is?"

"Because..." I close my eyes and take a deep breath. "Because he actually enjoys sex and relationships, and I don't...and that makes me feel like this awful, pathetic person."

My eyes are starting to sting behind my closed eyelids, but I said it. I finally said the truth out loud.

"You're not."

"Huh?" My eyes jolt open to see Wei gently looking back at me.

"Sly, you're not awful or pathetic. We here at Safe Space want to help you figure out how to live your most authentic life." He powers up the PC at the desk and begins typing. "It sounds like you already know who you are and what you like. Are you familiar with the terms 'asexual' or 'aromantic'?"

"Yes." I look down, my face feeling hot. "I think...that's what's wrong with me...I think I'm asexual."

"There's nothing wrong with you."

"There isn't?" I feel a small kindling of hope warm me up from the inside.

We spend the next twenty minutes discussing what it means to be asexual and aromantic. I relate so much to the experiences attributed to these labels. I'm not sure if I'm aromantic, but I definitely don't want a sexual relationship with anyone. It's a massive relief to know there are people out there who experience what I'm feeling. I turns out I am part of the broader queer umbrella. My mind is blown wide—QPU and Safe Space are a godsend.

Before I open the door to leave, Wei says, "And Sly? Just remember." I look right at him. "Your experiences and desires are your own. I couldn't change my orientation, and neither can you, and that's okay."

I smile at him and nod. "Wei, if I um...have any more questions, can I...?"

"Come by. You can reach out any time."

"Thanks. I definitely will." It warms my heart to know people like Simone and Wei are willing to help me out. Maybe there's hope for me after all. I haven't talked about my fear of being touched, but that's a problem for a different day. Being asexual—ace, for short—is a separate part of me, so I'm going to take this journey of self-discovery one day at a time.

I've been feeling better ever since my talk with Wei. The past week-and-a-half of play rehearsals have been challenging but fascinating. I feel myself slowly growing into the role of Dakin, as well as getting into the dramatic arts. We've mostly been doing deep dives into table-reading and characterizations, as well as touring the small stage. Today we finished up some light blocking, but most of the scenes didn't involve me, so I mainly sat around looking over my lines.

Aggie dismisses us for the evening, letting everyone know what to expect for the next rehearsal. "And next week we'll be doing physical work!" she announces. "So get ready to get close to your co-stars. I want to see sparks on stage. The sooner you get used to your fellow cast members' personal spaces, the better off we'll be. Enjoy your weekend!"

We leave, and I feel uncomfortable as I walk by my co-star Charles in the hallway. Aggie basically said we were going to start kissing next week, and the sheer thought of it makes me nauseous. Maybe I might be asexual, but I need to be convincing on stage. Everyone knows there's romance in *Izumi and Alex*, but I'm not sure if I'm ready to be physically close to someone like that. I have not-so-good memories of making out with my high school sort-of-but-not-really girlfriend. I know no one's asking me to have sex with Charles on stage, but tell that to my nerves and my lips.

The human oral orifice is chockful of germs—I'd like to keep mine to myself!

"So next week, huh?" Charles says. He's holding the straps of his backpack while walking beside me.

"Yup." I make a weird popping sound and look up at the ceiling. I think he's feeling as awkward as I am.

"It'll be no big deal. It's just acting."

"Yeah...theater life, what are you gonna do?" I shrug.

"Hey guys!" I turn to my right to see Omar running up to us, huffing. He has a distressed look on his face, but I'm not sure why. "What uh...what's up?"

"We were just talking about Monday," Charles says. "How we're going to need to get all up in each other's faces." He chuckles, and I force a short laugh as well.

"Yeah, but it's acting...just playing pretend,

right? Like...that's showbiz? Right?" Omar's waving around his hands frenetically while explaining this to us.

"Um, yeah," I reply.

"Sly and I got this," Charles says. We get to a fork in the hallway and he cocks his head left. "My car's parked down that way. Night, boys."

"Night," Omar and I reply. Soon enough, it's just him and me walking down a long corridor.

After a beat, Omar breaks the silence. "You feeling good to do blocking and physical work next week?"

"Mmm...I think so." I nod my head and look forward while we walk up the stairs. "I'm so new to all this."

"Bro, same." Omar laughs. "I need to get an A for this gig, but Aggie keeps throwing new terms at me and shit. I'm still trying to find out where 'stage left' is!" We both chuckle at that.

We get up the stairs and turn to a large corridor with spotlights and massive floor-to-ceiling windows peering into the courtyard. It's dark out, so all we see are our reflections and the various student artworks on the wall; I'm definitely where Steven asked me to meet him.

"Look, Sly, if you ever..." I turn to Omar who's looking right at me with his wide brown eyes. "If you ever need help going over lines, you can text me."

"Thanks," I reply with a smile. "That's very generous of you, Omar."

He smiles back, and I swear, he blushes. I'm about to ask him why he's acting so weird when I hear my name.

"Sly." We both turn to see my brother carrying a large piece of art on a black-board. "And Omar? What are you doing here?"

"I was just..." He turns to me and raises his eyebrows, urging me to jump in. I'm touched that he's letting me tell my brother the big news.

"I'm part of the school's fall musical production."

"No shit!" Steven beams at me. "That sounds pretty sweet."

"And Omar is the assistant director."

"Oh." Steven eyes him for a moment, his smile dimming a bit. "That's cool, too."

"Yeah. I should probably go," Omar says.

"I'm almost done here, putting up some pieces," my brother says, pointing at the art in his hand. "Sly and I will be leaving very soon. We might call our mom later." I feel like he's being dismissive to Omar, but I'm not sure why.

"Right." Omar scratches his head, looks down at the floor, then back at me. "Goodnight then. See you next week."

"Bye," I say with a wave. After he's gone, I turn to see Steven putting his art piece on the wall. He attaches some thumbtacks to each corner, then squints his eyes at it and tilts his head. "I didn't know we were calling Mom tonight."

"We can if you want. I have no preference. Hey, does this look crooked to you?" he asks.

"Uh, no."

"Good." He puts the final two tacks on. The silence in this massive hallway is giving me anxiety.

"Do you...not want me to be in the play or something?"

Steven turns and looks me up and down; his face has a veneer of judgment. "I think it's great that you're doing a play. Mom and Dad and everyone else will come up to see it, and that'll be awesome."

"So then...do you not like *Omar*? I thought you wanted me to make friends with your friends."

Steven turns back around and pushes in the thumbtacks some more. "Omar is Ravi's best friend. The four of them are a unit." Steven's voice bounces off the wall.

"Okay," I reply, waiting for him to clarify.

He steps back and looks his piece up and down, wiping his hands on his shirt. "It's just...Ravi tells me he's...Well, he gets around. A *lot*." Steven finally looks me in the eye. "He breaks guys' and girls' hearts all over town."

My eyebrows furrow. "That's his business and his alone."

Steven stares back at his artwork again and another moment of quiet passes. "You're right. It's not like you're trying to hook up with him. That'd be wrong, like soccer-team incest." He laughs but doesn't notice my frown. "Come on, car's this way."

I follow my brother down the hall, still unhappy with this latest conversation. Typical Steven, not respecting my decisions; I'm not trying to hook up with Omar, but so what if I was? He's my friend now. He's helpful and genuine, not to mention handsome. I could do a lot worse than him. Who cares if girls and guys fall for him and he turns them down? He has the prerogative to sleep around if he wants. He's probably still figuring himself out, just like me, and I don't need my brother's approval just to be friends with the guy.

11: Omar

I run out of the locker room into the summer air, still damp from the shower. We've just finished our first preseason home game, and we won, which was nice, but I don't stay to catch up with the guys. The game cut into play rehearsal, and I've got a lot on my plate. Aggie knows about my soccer commitments, and Coach Dacks knows about my unconventional class schedule; still, I still don't like to disappoint either of them. I may not have a career path in life, but I ride-or-die for my soccer boys.

I've also grown to really care about the musical I'm helping direct. This is in no small part thanks to a certain glasses-clad junior whom I can't seem to push out of my head. I refuse to admit I've caught feelings, but the idea of Sly getting close to his romantic co-star Charles makes me want to commit acts of violence.

I hear my inner voice say "*Get a grip, Omar. A relationship isn't for you.*"

I finally make it to the auditorium, panting and striding down the aisles. Several students are sitting around, some reading and others fiddling on their phones. Aggie is on stage, standing in front of the two female leads; they all have scripts in hand.

"Omar, good you're here."

"I'm sorry," I huff. "We had a soccer game."

"It doesn't matter, listen." She waves her hand to interrupt me. "I'm busy doing blocking with Tisha and Celia. I need you to go downstairs to Room B03. It's a dance room I've booked for rehearsal. I want you to take those two"—she points down to where Sly and Charles are chatting—"and run their lines and blocking for act three."

I blink at her and swallow nothing. "Um, act three?" I memorized this script, but I still need to hear her say it.

"Yes, I'm working with these two ladies now and getting them used to each other's spaces. I'm really solidifying their onstage chemistry. I need you to do the same. Run the scenes with Ezekiel and Dakin and get them used to the motions. I already explained this to Charles and Sylvester." She points down, and I see the two already getting up, gathering their belongings.

I gulp again. I have to be in a room with the two of them and direct them on how to be romantic? I didn't think I'd need to do all this so soon! "Um...can't we work on act one?"

"No, they can do that on their own. Now go, Omar, please. You were already late. I don't want to lose more time."

I nod and walk away. Aggie is right to be irritated; I'm supposed to be her right-hand man and I shouldn't be questioning her on this. It's not like she asked me anything complicated. I just have to go into a private room. With Charles and Sly. And watch them kiss. Easy, right?

"Okay, let's take it from the scene change," I announce. My voice bounces off the mirrored-walls in the large room. There's a massive linoleum floor that's primarily for dance majors, but tonight it's our private rehearsal space. "The lights go up and the stage now reveals a lush forest. This signals that Dakin has just gotten his magic back thanks to Ezekiel's help." I sit down on a backwards chair. I look left and right at Charles and Sly. They have their scripts in hand but shouldn't be using them. "And...action!"

"Fantastic!" Sly says in character. "Glorious! This is truly remarkable!"

"Indeed you are," Charles replies in character. He's supposed to look enamored, but he comes off as creepy. Maybe I'm just projecting, but I think he needs to tone it down. "You are the most remarkable fairy gentlesir I've ever seen."

"Have you seen many of my kind?" Sly asks, cocking an eyebrow. He has the flirtation down pat. It makes me wonder what it would be like to have him throw that my way.

"I don't need to. Dakin, you've done so much for me," Charles recites.

"It is you, Prince Ezekiel, who has saved me. You have allowed me to rediscover magic. I cannot thank you enough." He hesitates, then steps forward and puts his hand on Charles's face. "You make me believe again, Ezekiel. My feelings for you are so evident in this lush forest. 'Twas my magic, yes, but you were the spark that set my heart ablaze."

Charles puts his hand over Sly's and steps closer. It's the moment of truth; Charles leans in, towering over Sly. I don't really want to see them kiss, but I do want to see Ezekiel and Dakin kiss. Plus, I'm the assistant director, my grade is on the line, *yadda yadda yadda...*

Before their lips touch, I notice Sly stiffen in his arms. Charles is leaning in and Sly is pulling back, so obviously uncomfortable. Okay, this isn't helping anyone. "Cut!" I yell.

Sly immediately breaks off, stepping back from Charles's hold. "Alright," I announce. "It's okay to be nervous."

"I'm not nervous!" Sly barks. He turns back to Charles. "I swear I'm not," he says, softer this time.

"That's fine. Let's all take a deep breath." I inhale and exhale dramatically and watch them do the same. "Alright then, let's take that again from '*I don't need to, Dakin.*' And... action!"

The two actors get back into position, a few feet from each other. "I don't need to. Dakin, you've done so much for me," Charles recites again.

"It is you, Prince Ezekiel, who has saved me. You have allowed me to rediscover magic. I cannot thank you enough." Once again, Sly steps forward and puts his hand on Charles's face. "You make me believe again, Ezekiel. My feelings for you are so evident in this lush forest. 'Twas my magic, yes, but you..." Charles puts his hand over Sly's, and it's obvious Sly is trembling. I suddenly recall him mentioning he doesn't like being touched. I thought that wasn't going to be an issue for the play, but Sly looks like he's going to vomit if we keep going. "You uh...you were the uh spark...that...that set my heart ablaze."

Charles leans in, his mouth centimeters away from Sly's. I feel the tension in the room, and it's not romantic—it's just stressful. Just then, Sly pulls back, breaking free from Charles, and gasps for air.

"Okay! Okay," I announce, getting up and walking up to them. "Let's call it quits for the day. We don't need to do anymore."

"But Aggie said we need to run—"

"I'll work with Sly," I say, interrupting Charles. "On some scenes, I promise. Take the night off, Charles." He stares at me uncertainly, and then I turn to my right to see Sly hunched over. Charles can go fuck off. I need to make sure Sly is okay.

I get as close as I can to Sly without touching him. I see in the various mirrors Charles has walked away. *Good riddance.* "Hey...hey, Sly? It's me, Omar."

Sly finally stands up straight and nods his head. He's breathing deeply through his nose, and his eyes are still closed. "You uh...you alright?"

"It's my haphephobia," he mutters. I make a mental note to look it up, but I'm pretty sure it's a fear of being touched.

I want so badly to hold him. I want to take away all his anxieties and discomfort. I have no idea what it is about him, but looking out for him just feels right. "Forget about rehearsal tonight. Do you want to uh...go get food?"

He shakes his head and moves around like he just stubbed his toe. "No," he finally whispers. "I don't want anyone to see me like this."

"Um...I could walk you to your car?"

"I don't wanna go home right now." He continues to pace back and forth. "Too many lights...too much...stuff around me."

I nod and look around. An idea strikes me. "Come here." I

make sure not to touch him and guide him toward the far wall, next to the door. I shut the door and turn off two of the three lights. Now the room is darker, but the one light lets us see each other.

"Sit down," I whisper. I lean against the mirrored wall and lower myself down. For a moment, I think he's going to refuse, but he finally sits down next to me, inches separating us. His eyes are closed again, but at least now his chest isn't going up and down with force. "Good. Now breathe with me."

I take a deep three-second breath and Sly mimics me. I breathe out slowly and watch his whole body relax. "You don't have to go anywhere. No one else is here."

"Thank you," he whispers, eyes still shut. "I'm...so embarrassed. I can't believe—"

"You don't have to explain anything to me. Take your time." I want to tell him I'm not going anywhere, but that would be too much too soon. After a few seconds of silence, I finally say, "When I need to get out of my head, I watch romantic comedy TV shows. Wanna watch something dumb and cheesy?" This earns me a genuine grin and Sly opens his eyes.

"Sure," he replies, voice still hoarse. I smile at him, then whip out my phone and pull up my favorite sitcom.

Twenty-two minutes later, the credits are rolling and Sly and I haven't moved. We shared some laughs, and I can tell he's feeling less stressed than before. "You okay?" I ask.

Sly nods, then curls up, putting his head in his hands. "Ugh," he groans. "I'm the worst."

"No, no you're not!" I sit closer to him still; our thighs are touching.

"Yes, I am," he whines, his face still buried in his palms. "I can't even handle a simple stupid onstage kiss. How am I ever gonna make it in this play if I hate being touched?"

"Is it because of anything Charles did? Is it because he's a guy?" I pray it's the former, but that's a selfish thought, so I need to move past that.

"No...it would be the same if he was a girl. Ugh..." He moans again, and I instinctively put my hand on his back and rub his shoulder. When I realize it, I almost stop, but he doesn't flinch away.

"It's gonna be okay, man," I say, trying to comfort him

Sly raises his head and moves his neck, allowing me to rub his back up to his lower scalp. His eyes are shut, but a soft moan escapes his lips. Then it dawns on me: Sly is leaning into my touch!

"Sly...I don't want to alarm you."

"Hm?" he responds. His eyes are still shut and he's clearly enjoying my hand on his back.

"I've been touching you for like thirty seconds."

He opens his eyes at me. I think he's gonna break away or have another panic attack. Instead, he just looks at me with an expressionless stare. He definitely feels calmer than he did when he was rehearsing with Charles, so I'll take that as a compliment.

"I...guess you have been," he finally says.

I stop rubbing his back but leave my hand there. "We're really touchy-feely on the team. I think it's a sports thing. Do you want me to stop?"

"No, actually." He looks down like he's trying to solve a puzzle. He finally catches my gaze again. "Can you keep going?" His voice is firmer and more resolute now.

"Turn a little," I say. My voice bounces off the walls of the semi-lit room. If he were some random guy, I'd totally try to make a pass at him right now. But no, this is about making my new friend — my best friend's boyfriend's little brother — feel better.

He shifts and I scooch a little closer. This puts me in the perfect spot to put both hands on his shoulders, right next to his neck, and I start to massage him. He feels so tense, but he immediately relaxes as I work my fingers into him. I go at it for two minutes more, listening intently to the adorable — no, sexy — moans coming out of his mouth. I want him to feel like he didn't have a panic attack thirty minutes ago; I want Sly O'Rourke to feel good.

"How you doing?"

"Great, actually," he replies. He turns to look at me, and my hands slide off him. "You're...something else Omar."

I grin and shrug, looking up. "I get that a lot. Good or bad, I'm definitely something else."

"I'm serious. Um...thank you."

"Don't mention it." We share a smile.

He looks down and makes that pondering face again. The momentary urge to kiss him flashes through me and I remind myself I can only care for him like a brother. "I really hate being touched."

"Oh?" I ask, not sure how to respond.

"You scared me that day...during the cake incident...but the first night we met, you touched my face..."

"Sorry about that." I cringe.

"No, what I'm trying to say is...it wasn't even that bad? When it's you, it's like I don't mind." He looks back up, his brown eyes catching mine. He has a gorgeous face with smooth skin, and perfectly-styled brown hair. "What is it

67

about...*you?*"

My heart is beating out of my chest, and I lick my lips on instinct. Before I can respond, Sly says, "I bet it's 'cause you're tight with my brother. That makes me like a brother to you. Transitive property, remember?"

He smiles at me, and I melt at the sight. I feel hope and disappointment clash in my chest—Sly has friend-zoned me, but this is what I wanted, right?

"Maybe...to help for the play, we can practice...physical contact? Just you and me?" His huge brown eyes are filled with need, but I'm frozen with conflict. Is he asking me what I think he's asking?

When I don't respond after a few seconds, he says "I'm sorry. That was inappropriate."

"No!" I blurt. He raises his eyebrows and I tear my eyes off him and look around. Our reflections are infinitely bouncing off the mirrored walls. "It...could be arranged."

When I look back at Sly, he's got that million-dollar smile on. He raises his hand for a handshake. "So...you don't mind helping me get over my fear of being touched? As friends, in private?"

I gulp. Being in a secluded room and putting my hands—and who knows what else—on Sly's body? This is a disaster waiting to happen. I've read enough romance novels and screenplays to know that this can only lead to catching even more feelings and heartbreak. *Bad idea, Omar. Pull back now.*

I hear my own voice before I register I'm saying it. "When do you wanna start?"

12: Sly

I *will* get over my fear of physical contact if it's the last thing I do. Going away to college is all about discovering yourself, right? Well, with Omar's help, I'm going to discover the *crap* out of myself and enjoy being touched.

I don't know what it is about him; when he's not sneaking up on me while I'm eating cake, I don't actually mind being near him. He's comforting, friendly, and we get along great. We chat during rehearsal, text on occasion, exchanging random theater memes. Overall, he's such a good guy. He might be the person I've grown closest to at KU, other than Wei. On top of that, his massage the other day felt pretty good.

Before coming to KU, the idea of a full body massage felt like a nightmare, but now? I'd be down to let Omar do that. I'd even be willing to return the favor. The idea of putting my hands on his chiseled back while he's face down wearing nothing is *not* horrifying. Instead, the thought makes me feel...dizzy for some reason.

Speaking of favors, today I'm outside his dorm trying to play it cool while I hold a bag filled with breakfast.

Since Omar is helping me out, the least I can do is repay him in carbs. He texts me that he's on his way downstairs, and sixty seconds later, he's at the door. He's wearing a white tank top and plaid pajama pants; he looks comfy. He definitely just rolled out of bed, and I appreciate it immensely that he's willing to work with me on play rehearsal stuff in private.

"How's it going?" he asks while we walk up the stairs.

"I'm great. Pumped. Got you a raisin bagel with chive cream cheese, just like you asked, even though that's gross."

"Yes!" he replies, pumping a fist in the air, and I can't help but giggle.

We make it to his suite, and no one's around in the common room—good, I want to be as discreet as possible. He guides me to his room, and I'm taken aback by how neat it is. The sheets are plaid and perfectly kept on the bed, and there's nary a sock on the floor.

"You can have a seat," Omar says, pointing to his desk chair. He pulls in a small chair from the common room and closes the door. Pretty soon, we're both sitting down munching on bagels.

"How are you liking Korham's food so far?" Omar asks in between bites.

"Good. I got plain cream cheese on a wheat bagel, because I'm boring."

He chuckles in response. We're back to eating in silence. It's not uncomfortable, but there's so much I want to tell him.

"It's not just my haphephobia. I should probably explain why physical contact makes me uncomfortable."

"You don't have to," Omar replies. That's sweet of him.

"But I want to. You're helping me out so much, and this might make it clearer for you...knowing why I *am* the way I am. You promise not to tell anyone?"

"Dude, this is a private off-the-book rehearsal where we're going to practice touching each other." He grins at me. "We have to keep it all secret."

"That's true." I take a swig of water then wipe my mouth with the back of my hand. I'm staring at the desk suddenly nervous. *Just out with it, Sly.* "I've been doing a lot of self-reflection, and...I think I'm asexual."

"Oh. Okay." Omar sucks the remnants of the cream cheese from his thumb and uses some hand-sanitizer to wipe it all off. "You need some sanitizer?"

I nod, and he applies some of the clear liquid to my hands. "Did you hear what I said?"

"You said you think you're asexual." He shrugs like I didn't just drop this massive bombshell.

"And doesn't that...weird you out?"

"Why would it weird me out? We all get to define ourselves. I'm bi, Ravi's gay, Kareem's straight, and you're ace. That's your label. Your journey." He stands up and smooths the covers on his already neat bed. "You ready to have a seat here?"

I'm so dumbfounded, but I stand up anyway and crawl onto the elevated bed. I'm now sitting with my back on the wall next to Omar. He's smiling at me and wiggling his dangling feet. He's adorable, anyone can see that, but the fact that he's so accepting of my orientation is insanely attractive. I understand why all the guys and girls fall for him.

We both stare at each other and laugh out of awkwardness. "So..." he says in a tone that's urging me to take the lead.

"Is it embarrassing to say I have a list on my phone starting from innocent things and leading up to kissing?" I pull out my phone, and Omar giggles.

"Nah, man. Casa de Omar is a judgment-free zone." His smile is making me dizzy, so instead, I focus on my list.

"Okay. Number one: hand-holding."

"Alright." Omar dangles his hand over mine, and I stare at it. The usual prickle of anxiety before a handshake is gone. "Sly?" I look up at his deep brown eyes. He's got a night's growth of stubble defining his strong jaw. This attractive soccer jock is in bed with me, and we're about to practice holding hands.

My life is somehow insane and boring in equal measure.

"You ready?" Omar asks.

I clear my throat. "I think so."

"If you need us to stop, just say 'stop.'"

"Like a safe word?"

"Exactly, except less kinky," he says, grinning.

"I don't know, man. Hand-holding can be *a real turn-on*." I'm joking, but Omar's smile falls just for a moment, his eyes darting lower on my face.

"It is for me too. I love it. It's such an intimate expression of..." His voice is deeper, but I'm not sure why. After a moment, he clears his throat and is back to smiling. "Anyway, you need to be the one to initiate. Go for it, Sly."

I put my hand under his and lace our fingers

together. His hand is warm and comforting—I like it.

"Alright. How are you feeling?"

"Good. Touching Charles's hand doesn't really affect me."

"Okay, well..." Omar pulls his hand off. "What's next?"

I look down at my list. "Side-hugging?"

"Sure...a little over-the-shoulder hug action. May I?" He wags his eyebrows and I chuckle.

"Consent granted." I smile, and he slowly reaches over his right side. His hand is now perched on my right shoulder—I don't feel a thing. It's not like at the party, because this time I see it coming. More importantly, Omar's my friend. I've never felt so comfortable with someone, physically or friendship-wise. Omar Odom makes me feel safe.

"You good?"

"Uh...yeah," I reply. There's space between us on the bed and I scooch closer.

"You can...put your head on my shoulder." I do as I'm told. I'm now full-on cuddling Omar Odom on his bed, and I don't hate it. No, it actually feels kind of nice. He's warm, and I'm getting this tingling sensation from my toes up to my head.

"You good, Sly?" His voice is deep and reverberates through my side. Hearing him say my name feels like a jolt in my heart. Omar smells damn good too. His body is comforting, and his smooth skin on mine makes me feel... something I'm unfamiliar with.

"You want me to stop?" I look up at him, his face so close to mine. In this light, his skin is an ochre complexion, and his full lips are framed by pristine dark stubble. If he could just lean in, we'd be sharing a breath. But…wanting him to kiss me…that means that I'm not…

Nope. No way. I just got to understand myself. I'm not even going to entertain the idea that I'm not asexual.

I push off him and leap off the bed and laugh awkwardly. "Okay! Ha ha…"

"What's wrong?" Omar asks, rightfully confused. "Did I do something?"

"No! But I uh…I think we've made some progress today!" I'm hopping up and down, trying to get my shoes on. "We're…we're good for now." I'm stammering, laughing and wobbling, all while trying to stuff my feet into my shoes.

"Okay," Omar says. He gets up and his face is etched with concern. "If you think we're done for today, then I guess I'll see you…"

"Yup!" I yelp in a voice an octave higher than I usually use. "Later, Alligator!" *Why do I keep saying that?* I bolt out the door and cringe at my stupid nickname.

Once I get out of his building, I finally take a full breath. I jog to my car breathing in the late September air. *What is wrong with me?* I've never had a physical reaction other than disgust with anyone before, certainly not with a dude. Life would be so much easier if I was clearly gay, like my brother, but I'm not. Being intimate, kissing, getting to second and all the other bases with another person is *not* for me.

Then why can I still feel Omar's warm body by my side? And why do I have visions of kissing him, touching him, and removing all of our clothes until I'm covering my body with his? What the *hell* is happening to me?

13: Omar

"Great work out there! Another W in the books!" Kareem shouts. A few people on the team cheer in the locker room as he walks by and fist-bumps Landon and me.

"You know it." I smile and put on the rest of my clothes. Once I check the time on my phone, I panic—I'm hella late for play rehearsal. Our game went a little longer than usual, and Aggie knows I'm here, but I still need to get there now.

"You getting food with us?" Ravi asks.

"Can't. Rehearsal."

"Seriously? I feel like you're always there!" Kareem adds.

"Yeah, well, it's a class," I throw back.

"Damn, those must be some huge credits you're earning," Landon says while putting on a shirt.

"For sure. Peace." I leave, but not before noticing the extreme disappointment on Kareem's face. I try to ignore it so I can focus on what needs to get done today at rehearsal.

The show is really coming together. The past

three weeks I've been learning so much about directing, costume design, lighting, and everything that goes into producing a real show. I've gotten to work with painting the sets, coordinating the different stage hand teams, and becoming entrenched in all things *Izumi and Alex*. There's a warmth I feel inside whenever a scene goes well or Aggie praises me on my set decisions. It's similar to when we win against a particularly skilled team—it's a sense of accomplishment.

When people say "pursue your passions," is *this* what they're talking about?

At rehearsal, we go through a lot of blocking, and I can tell the actors are really growing into their characters. I'm spending most of today in the sound and lighting booth, and I watch as Tisha and Celia make sparks fly on stage.

Unfortunately, I can't say the same about Charles and Sly. We haven't had another 'touchy-handsy fun time' since that first session. I've barely gotten to talk to him because I've been so focused on my other classes and soccer, so I don't know how he's feeling. I'm honored that he confided in me that he's asexual, and I'm a bit relieved; it's much easier to friend-zone him knowing he doesn't want any sex or feelings from me.

Today, however, he's all stiff in Charles's arms on stage. He's not panicking when he puts his lips on his co-star, but I can tell Sly really doesn't want it. I understand he's ace, but I thought we'd worked on his touch aversion? Clearly we haven't progressed enough, because after two takes, Aggie is yelling "Cut! Take five, everyone!"

I dash down the stairs to get to where Sly is. I

don't want Aggie to tear him a new one, so if I can intercept in any way, I will. As usual, I don't know why; I just know I need to look out for him.

Once I get there, Aggie is done talking and the three of them are parting ways. "What's up?" I ask Sly, catching my breath.

He looks defeated as he pushes his glasses up. "Oh, nothing. Aggie basically just said she's seen dead trees with more romantic chemistry than us, that's all." His shoulders slump as he walks away.

"Why don't you practice it now?"

Sly grimaces. "Aggie is going to go work with some chorus line people on act one. She wants us to run lines by ourselves but..." He looks left and right, but there's no one near us. "I kinda just want to be alone. Having to kiss on stage has made my asexual ass tired."

"Ah." I look down and bounce on my heels.

"You haven't told anyone about my orientation, right?"

"No! Never."

"Okay." He goes back to slumping his shoulders, giving his best sad donkey impression. "Well...see ya."

"Maybe you and I should practice more?" I ask quickly. "In private?"

Sly stares at me. I can see the fear, doubt, and hope in his eyes past his glasses. "Are you sure?"

"Of course! For the good of the play."

"Right." He nods slowly. "For the play."

A grin slowly spreads on my face. "And I'm looking out for you. Anything to help you." I tap his shoulder with my rolled-up script. "Little O'Rourke."

He grins and looks up. "I hate that nickname."

"Hey, it's fair play since you nicknamed me 'Alligator.'" I smile.

"Hey! That was...not..."

"Nope! Too late. That's the rule of nicknames."

"It is?" He chuckles.

"Yes, according to the bylaws of soccer." I beam at him and he already seems more at ease. "I'm free next Sunday morning. I'll probably be super tired, but it's nothing a chive-cream-cheese-on-a-raisin-bagel can't fix!"

"That's still gross, man," he says, fighting a grin.

"Alligators will eat anything." I wag my eyebrows, and he chuckles. I'll do anything to make him smile again. "So Sunday?"

He shrugs. "I guess it can't hurt to try again."

"Atta boy." I wink at him for good measure, then step back. I'm counting the hours until next Sunday.

14: Sly

I see the door to the QPU room is open, which means no one is there for office hours. I stride in without looking up and loudly say, "You told me I was *ASEXUAL*! And now look at me!" This is a mistake, because, once I lift my head up, I see Wei at his desk. And he's not alone. That tall, broad-shouldered man is sitting on his desk. They're extremely close, and now they both turn to me, eyebrows raised.

Oops. Maybe I should have knocked first.

"Uhh..." I say, my face probably pale white.

"Uh...hi Sly!" Wei says, a panic in his voice. "Mr. Micucci was just leaving!"

Logan stands up and straightens out the wrinkles on his tight polo. "Yes!" He clears his throat and turns to Wei. "You told me no one comes to office hours!" he whispers loudly.

"I said, 'sometimes I'm alone,' and you took that as an invitation!" Wei whispers back in an angry tone.

"Um, should I go?" I ask.

"No!" they say in unison, once again looking at

me.

"Swing by later," Logan whispers to Wei, winking at him. They're both grinning as he turns to walk away. "I didn't hear anything," he says to me without stopping. He closes the door, and now it's just me and Wei.

"Sorry about that."

"It's cool," I reply. I grab a chair and sit across from him.

"Welcome to QPU Safe Space. My name is—"

"Yeah, yeah." I wave my hand to cut him off. "Listen, Wei, I need your help."

"Shoot," he says, nodding. His eyes are kind and welcoming, and I know I came to the right person.

"Look." I take a deep breath and stare at the floor. "When I left here last time, I thought I was...asexual."

"Okay."

"But now there's been...a development." That's one way to describe the gorgeous bisexual jock whose hands made me feel at ease for the first time ever.

"Do you want to elaborate?" Wei asks.

"There's...this...guy." I look up and see Wei urging me to continue with his eyes. "We've been...hanging out...and it's like...when he touches me I'm on fire."

"Is he hurting you?"

"No!" I quickly correct him. My eyes hit the floor again. "It's not like that. When I'm around him, my heart beats faster. The thought of him putting his arm around mine...it feels nice. And the idea of kissing him or doing...more intimate things...It's not gross."

"Okay..." Wei says.

"I think I would actually want that. Being...intimate. And he might want me, too."

"I don't see the problem. As long as you're both consenting adults."

"The problem is I'm ace," I exclaim, looking back at him. "I thought that was it, and I was done discovering myself!"

Wei gives me a sympathetic look. "There is no timetable or end date for these kinds of things. And there's no catch-all label for every person with the feelings you're experiencing. Sly, you're a young man; you're still going through all these changes, and if you discover new things about yourself now or for decades to come, that's okay, too."

"But I don't *want* to discover new things about myself," I whine. "I finally found a label that fits me. I don't want to complicate things."

"Alright," Wei says. "Well, think about this person on your mind. What do you want when he's around?"

I imagine Omar's perfect body and gorgeous face. I dwell on his warm brown eyes and comforting voice. Then I think about him sweaty...taking off his shirt...and then he takes off *my* shirt...and then we...

"*Fuck,*" I whisper.

"Pardon?"

"I mean uh..." I say louder. "I was just considering the possibility that..." I roll my shoulders. "I just thought asexual people didn't have these kinds of feelings, that's all."

"Well, sexualities and orientations are complex." Wei turns on his PC. "Have you heard of gray-asexuality?"

"What?"

For the next twenty minutes, Wei shows me online research for all sorts of labels I've never heard of. I had no idea there were subsets underneath subsets of sexualities! Gray-ace...demisexual... A lot of these labels can partially define my experiences, and I'm equal parts relieved and perplexed.

I thought it was just gay, straight, or bi—so glad I came to this university to broaden my views!

As I leave, I thank Wei one more time. "I hope things work out with...whomever you're referring to."

"Thanks." We smile at each other. "Can I call you sometime for more advice?"

"Of course! Ravi and the boys helped me out a lot last semester, so we're all friends. I want to pay it forward for Ravi's boyfriend's little brother." Wei smiles at me, and I'm touched.

I nod and walk away, dwelling on his final words: *Ravi's boyfriend's little brother.* I pray that's not all I am to Omar. I hope he thinks of me as someone worth kissing or doing more with.

Early Sunday morning, Omar lets me into his building, wearing the same white tank top and plaid pajama pants as before. I carry a bag of bagels as he guides me into his suite, and I'm once again relieved no one else sees us. We chat for a bit about nothing important as he locks his door and I take one of the two seats.

He sits down at his desk and is about to take a bite of his bagel when he sees me staring at him.

"What?" he asks, his food hovering below his mouth.

"Do...did...do you..." I'm stuttering and starting

to sweat. I've never been uncomfortable with Omar before. Why now? *Just out with it, Sly.* "Did you...brush your teeth already?"

Omar's eyebrows furrow. "Huh?"

"Never mind."

"Are you saying my breath smells bad?" He puts down the food, blows into his hands, and takes a sniff.

"No! Never! I just..." My shoulders tense up, and I look at the ceiling. "I thought maybe we could try kissing today, that's all."

"Oh...oh!" Omar gets up and smooths the covers on his bed. I'm reminded of sitting there the last time, how aroused it got me and how I'll be headed straight there again in two seconds. "Um...yeah...if that's on your list."

"It's to help with the play!" I blurt, getting up and toeing off my shoes.

"Of course. And you have no problem with... with kissing me?" He's stuttering now, too. *Is he just as nervous as me?*

"No! Absolutely not. Do...you have a problem with kissing me?"

"Nope!" He hops on the bed, and I follow suit. A moment later, I'm sitting up, back against the wall, right next to him again. *Heaven help me; he smells good.* "I just wanna be considerate of you...'cause you're ace."

"Right yeah...and we're friends," I remark.

"Bros even."

"Totally. And it's practice for the play!"

"Exactly!"

"And you're Omar; it's not like you'll catch feelings."

"Nope!" he yelps, still not making eye contact

with me. "And you're Sly; you're ace, and this is strictly business." We're both speaking quickly now.

"Absolutely. Just business." I put out my hand for him to shake, and he smiles and takes it.

As he shakes my hand, I stare at his perfect face. He's gazing back at me with those huge brown eyes. My pulse doubles, and my mouth goes dry. Okay, there's no denying it—I'm so attracted to Omar, the soccer jock.

Just as I'm thinking this, his smile fades and his eyes dart down to my lips. "*Just like in the movies!*" I think to myself. Right before...

Ah, screw it.

I pull my arm back, and since I'm gripping his huge hand, he juts forward. I catch his lips with mine, and it feels like an earthquake in my heart. His mouth is soft, his stubble tickles, and when he puts his hand on my cheek, everything just feels right.

Kissing has *never* felt like this.

His lips part, and I follow his lead, allowing my tongue to greet his mouth. When Omar moans into me, that earthquake from before makes way for a volcano. His mouth massages mine, his groans vibrate into me, and I love it. *Fuck*, this is hot, and I'll do anything to feel it again.

I've never been attracted to anyone before, not the way I am to Omar. This feels *nothing* like kissing Charles or any girl for that matter. Screw the past. I'm going to say this was my first kiss years from now.

After a blazing hot eternity, we break apart. When I open my eyes, he's finally opening his.

"Woah," he says in a breathy whisper.

"Did I do good?" I smirk, knowing the answer.

"I was gonna ask...are you *sure* you need

practice kissing? Because that was…" He shakes his head smiling. "Wow."

"That was 'wow'? You have a way with words, Alligator." I'm grinning, satisfied with the knowledge we both enjoyed that kiss.

"But how was it for you?"

"Hmm, well, I think I need more practicing." I grab his face and swiftly guide his mouth back to mine. This time, I moan into him as his tongue explores my mouth. He feels, tastes, and smells so delightful. Is *this* what everyone's been hyped up about all these years? Kissing was so boring before, but this? This is next level.

Now I understand the phrase "one thing led to another," because making out with Omar has me wanting to rip off every fiber of clothing between us.

It takes all my willpower to pull back. He's smiling, trying to catch his breath, and I refuse to acknowledge the tent in his pajama pants. *Baby steps, Sly.*

"That was…something else," Omar says.

"*You're* something else, Omar." I'm rubbing his cheek, counting the seconds until I get to do that again.

"But seriously, how was it? Did it feel like kissing on stage?" I almost roll my eyes, but, of course, we're here under the pretense of play rehearsal. A tiny seed of disappointment grows in my stomach, but I'm enjoying my time in bed with Omar. Now's not the time to be sad that the most promiscuous dude on the soccer team doesn't wanna be romantic with me. "Did it feel like kissing Charles?"

"No!" I yelp. "I mean…no."

"Oh, then what's different?" He still has his hands on either side of my neck, like he's as ready as I am to continue making out again.

"I don't know." I look down, then a grin grows on my face. I stare back into his precious brown eyes. "Let's try again and find out," I purr.

Once again, Omar and I assault each other's mouths. In bed. If this is what college self-discovery tastes like, I'm not going to complain.

After another minute or so of kissing, Omar pries his lips off mine to catch a breath and whip his tank top off. I've never cared about the male body before now, but I can't help but admire Omar; he's lean, chiseled, with perfect abs, and has chest hair in all the right places. He kisses me again, this time leaning his whole body into it. Now I'm splayed on his bed with this soccer jock's half-naked body on top of mine.

He puts his hand under my shirt, and I'm starting to feel claustrophobic again. I push up on my elbows and he breaks away from my lips. He looks flustered in the best way; his lips are a darker shade of pink and he's still devastatingly handsome.

"What's up?" Omar asks, his mouth quirking up in a half-smile.

"Nothing," I say, trying to ignore the obvious tent in his pants.

"Shit, did I go too far?"

"No, no, it's cool." I try to laugh it off and rotate my body so I'm leaning off the edge of his bed. "I was just…I've…I've never done anything more, so…" I'm stammering, looking down at the floor while my feet dangle.

"Shit," he hisses. He gets up and grabs his discarded shirt. "I am so sorry. Look at me, taking off my shirt, like a fucking horny idiot."

"Omar." I try to get his attention, but he ignores me.

"I can't even control myself," he mutters, pulling his tank

top over his head. "You're ace, so this is *so* messed up. This is supposed to be about play rehearsal, about me helping you... not fucking taking advantage of you. Shit, I'm the *worst*."

"Omar!" I stand up, and he looks at me, finally pausing. "It's fine. You're not taking advantage of me."

The look on his face is one of complete remorse. His huge brown eyes are tender, and I want to hold him again and tell him we're alright. He bites his lip, looks down, and then finally says "I think...we should call it a day. I need to cool off."

"Alright," I reply. I'm equal parts relieved and disappointed. I cross him to get to the door to leave, taking my breakfast with me. When I reach the doorknob, I turn back to him. "Just so you know, I learned there are different degrees to being ace. Gray-ace, demisexual, and other subsets."

He stares at me. "What does that mean for you?"

"That means..." I look down to choose my words carefully. "I've never had sex. Never wanted it. It's a boundary of mine, but...with you...things feel different Omar."

I look up and notice his eyebrows are raised. "If you ever wanna help me...learn about myself...and push my boundaries..." I smile at him for good measure, hoping I look sexy. "Just text me later, Alligator. Because I really liked kissing you."

I don't think I can handle any more rejection right now, so I push open the door and leave. The ball's in Omar's court, and I really hope he's down for an encore performance.

15: Omar

"You're just gonna hang out here alone?" Kareem asks, adjusting his superhero costume. It's Halloween night, and everyone else in my suite is preparing to go downtown to Steven's friends' house party.

"Yeah, man. I got some popcorn, some spooky movies, so I'm good." I'm sitting on the living room couch with my legs crossed on the table. I've donned a large green onesie with a cartoon alligator-head-hoodie. I was inspired by a certain someone with kind eyes and soft, perfect lips.

"Uh...okay." Kareem looks concerned, like he wants to convince me more. When Paul and Vince walk out wearing their super suits, they motion for him to head out. "Later, man."

"Have fun, boys!" I holler. Once they're gone, I stand up and take my hottest full-body selfie—as sexy as one can be in a cartoon onesie. It's been a week since I was in bed getting handsy with Sly, taking things way too far. He mentioned during one of our rehearsal breaks that he's not doing anything for Halloween, so I'm sending him this ridiculous pic of me. I hope he finds it hot or, at least, cute.

If I could get him to come over, maybe I can show him that I can restrain myself in his presence, that I'm more than just a fuckboy jock. Though the way he felt on my lips...Shit, he was addictive.

After ten long seconds, he responds to my text.

Sly: *Lol, cute, but what are you supposed to be? A dinosaur?*

Me: *Alligator.* (winky face)

Me: *What are you doing tonight? I'm alone and bored.*

Sly: *I was just gonna read in the library. I'm a real wild-child.*

Me: *Wanna come over and watch a scary movie?*

Sly: *Didn't you go out?*

Me: *Didn't want to. And now I'm a sad, lonely Alligator.*

Me: (another selfie of me pouting in costume)

Sly: *I don't really do scary movies.*

Me: *We can switch to rom-coms. I have popcorn!*

Sly: *Deal.*

Sly: *But only because I love popcorn.*

Fifteen minutes later, he texts me saying he's downstairs. I nearly stumble as I dash out the door. The smell of body spray and air freshener permeates the hallway, but most of that was me; I want to be clean all over in case Sly is serious about doing more than just kissing. I am totally down to have him rip this onesie to shreds if we're in bed.

After letting him in and guiding him up the stairs, I ask, "No costume?"

"I'm not going out," he replies. "Besides, I'm wearing an orange T-shirt."

"Oh well *excuse* me," I say. "Tone down the costume changes there, RuPaul."

"You can say I'm a pumpkin." I can hear his grin as we walk in and sit on the couch.

I turn on the TV to a low volume and put on some romantic comedy I've watched a hundred times. There's nothing between us on the couch except three inches of space. Out of the corner of my eye, I take in how handsome Sly looks tonight. His orange polo shirt hugs his tight little belly in all the right ways. His brown hair is slicked back and I want to taste the corners of his perfect mouth.

Shit. Now the nerves are starting to settle in, which is weird because I never get nervous before I fool around with anyone. "Popcorn?" I ask, passing him the bowl.

"Great." He takes it, pops some kernels in his mouth and places the bowl back on the table. I know the TV is playing, but it still feels so damn quiet. I need to say something. Sly puts me out of my misery when he clears his throat and says, "I like your costume."

"Thanks," I reply, my face getting warmer. I unzip the front a little more so my chest is showing. "It's a little warm but..."

"Alligator, huh?"

"What can I say?" I shrug. "This guy I know gave me this nickname, so now I'm partial to it." We both chuckle, and I stretch my arm over the couch until my hand is achingly close to his neck. I want so badly to make a move, but no. He's touch averse and gray-ace, which means I want him to be sure of any moves we make. Whatever's happening between us, Sly needs to take the lead, no matter how horny I am.

Just as I'm thinking that, I notice him looking at me.

Specifically, he's staring at the open slit on my costume revealing my chest. There's no doubt about it—he's attracted to me.

"Sly?"

"Hm?" he asks.

"My eyes...are up here." I unzip the onesie even further and smirk, knowing I've caught him.

"Uh..." His eyes are filled with conflict, darting up and down my body.

"How are you feeling about being gray-asexual? I haven't asked you about it, but I know orientations can be complicated."

"I'm uh..." He runs his hands through his hair. "I'm starting to understand it all, so I'm good."

"Great," I reply.

"It's like sometimes I want to try *some sex* things, but a lot of the time, I don't."

"Awesome."

"I've never experimented before, but at some point, I might want to."

"Got it."

"Like right now, I want to tear that ridiculous onesie off of you and put my mouth all over your body."

"Exactly. Wait, what?"

The next thing I know, Sly is straddling me, his face so close to mine. He's a firm weight, with both knees on the couch on either side of me, but I'm not stopping him. *Fuck,* this is hot and exactly how I wanted tonight to go.

"Omar..." he purrs, centimeters away from my face. As he speaks, his breath mingles with mine. "I enjoyed kissing you. Shit, I've been thinking about it for days."

"Really?"

"I want..." He gulps. "I want to try doing more...with you."

"Sly," I whisper. I'm trying to form words, but all the blood in my brain is currently down south. "Last time..."

"Last time, you were going too fast. But this time..." He starts to unzip my onesie further down, slower than candle wax melting on a warm day. "This time I'm in control. And I can go as slow...or as fast...as I want."

"I'm down." I chuckle, my breath dancing on his face. We're both grinning, but as I reach up to kiss his lips, he pulls back, just enough to have me nipping at the air. He's teasing me, but damn this is hot.

I'm usually a straight-to-business type of lover—I should have tried this edging foreplay stuff years ago!

I shift to a serious approach. "Sly, you have to tell me what you want. I want you to take the lead. You're new at this."

"That's very sweet of you." He kisses me on the cheek, then whispers into my ear, "Bedroom, Alligator?" Before I can reply, he leaps off me, and I follow him, adjusting the massive tent my boner is causing in my green costume. Sly O'Rourke has me wrapped around his little finger, and I'll willingly go wherever he wants to take me.

16: Sly

So this is what being horny for another person is like, huh? What a thrilling experience.

Omar locks the door and asks, "Okay, so what do you wanna do?" He unzips and drops his onesie and— *fuck*! I knew he was a lean soccer player, but as he stands there in just his plaid boxers, I can see how fit he is. He's all muscle and sinew, and while I appreciated the human form in the past, with Omar, it's dead sexy. He has me wanting so much, but only with him.

Being near Omar is like a passionate burst of red on the colorless canvas that has been my life thus far.

"Uh...Bed?" I shuck off my shirt, trying not to feel self-conscious about my wiry frame.

"Bet," Omar replies. He eyes me the way a little kid stares at a birthday cake. He hops up on the mattress in just his underwear and socks, and I try not to drool.

The idea of him getting handsy gives me mild anxiety, so I get creative. "I was thinking..." I whip off my belt and roll it up in my hands. "I could use this to maybe...

tie you up? A little? If that's okay with you?"

Omar looks like I just burst into flames. I'm about to apologize when he whispers, "Hell yeah."

"Really?"

"I don't know if this is a gray-ace thing, but it's kinky and I like it!" We both laugh, and he lies back, pulling his hands up and together. I hop up and, sixty seconds later, his wrists are tied.

"Now, they're a little loose because I'm not like, a cop. I don't want to subdue you. I know you would never hurt me but..."

"Sly, you don't have to apologize." His eyes are comforting, like always, but filled with passion and hope. "If you feel more at ease with this, then let's do it. I promise I'll let you know if I want you to stop."

I breathe a sigh of relief and pull my jeans off. "Oh good. I'm all about boundaries, so..."

"Then get over here and let's start defining those boundaries!" He wiggles and thrusts with the obvious erection in his boxers. "Please?"

I giggle and hop over him, straddling him once again. I finally lean in and capture his mouth with mine. He tastes so good, and this full-body contact feels electric. It's not at all disgusting—it feels right for once. Our crotches rub against each other, thin layers of fabric in the way, and now I'm just as hard as he is.

No one's ever felt my hard dick before, so this is a huge milestone for me.

I kiss down his neck, and he once again moans in delight. I guide my fingers down his perfect abs and happy trail. Soon enough, I'm at the waistband of his shorts. "Can I...pull this off?"

"Please do," he whispers. His eyes are rolling back, and with his hands bound above him, it looks like he's being tortured, but in a sexy way.

I drag his boxers down, and his hard cock springs out. I've never wanted to stare at another guy's junk, let alone play with one. But Omar lying here, hard as a rock for me? Oh yeah, that's making my blood boil. I finally know what it's like to truly be "turned on" for someone else.

I get back down to licking and sucking his neck. He moans and squirms, and none of my stupid anxiety motions are making an appearance, so I chase the moment. I go back to kissing his perfect mouth, and his lips are along for the ride. Pulling off, I ask, "Omar, can I...?"

"What? What do you want, babe?" he asks, breathlessly. His use of the word *'babe'* has my heart fluttering with visions of a happy future, but I block it out.

"Can I...jerk you off?"

He bites his lip and eyes me with a dark, intense stare. "On one condition...if you're cool with it."

"What?"

"Both of us. Jerk both of us at the same time. Rub against me."

"Seriously?" My dick is down for this plan, but I'm going to need more details.

"Yeah. It's called frotting and it would be so *so* hot." He bites his lip again and I'm starting to realize I'll do anything to please him. "Only if you're comfortable with it, though. If not..."

I flop over and pull my boxer briefs off before I can overthink it. The old Sly would never, but Omar is showing me all sorts of things about myself. A second later, my naked body is covering his, and our dicks are lined up.

I'm about to have sex, sort of. Holy shit.

I reach down and grasp us both, making his hips buck forward. His length is warm and pulses against mine. He's longer and thicker than me, but considering Omar's eyes keep rolling back, I don't think he cares. Finally, I put him out of his misery by stroking and thrusting back at him.

Fuck.

Fucccckkkk.

I know I'm the last person to realize this, but sex feels *amazing.*

I feel these warm sensations from my toes to my head. Each little grunt and whimper from Omar sends jolts of pleasure straight into my cock. Just knowing he's under me, bound up, and I'm in control of his pleasure...It's incredible.

We're both leaking like crazy, and I can't help but moan into his neck. He tastes so good, and my cock is in heaven right now. I need to know Omar feels just as good. "Fuck Sly," he gasps. "Faster...Please, I'm gonna..." Omar's breathy words are like music to my ears.

Seeing him lost in sexual bliss, with his perfect chin jutting upward, pushes me over the edge. I kiss the side of his mouth one last time and groan, exploding all over him. This orgasm is so hot, and I just keep blasting onto his abs. I've never shot this much before...No wait, that's Omar shooting, too.

Fuck. I did that for him. I did that for *us.*

After we're both done, I collapse next to him, eyes closed. I take a deep breath, wafting through a dream-like euphoric haze as my heartbeat slows down to normal. Now that the post-nut clarity is settling in, I feel...at peace? Not regretful, not anxious. I'm always overanalyzing everything, so self-conscious, afraid of every moment of physical contact. But now? I just got naked and shared an orgasm with a sexy soccer jock, and I fucking loved it.

"How are you doing, babe?" Omar whispers. I open my eyes to see him, still bound up, but eyeing me intensely. He looks concerned, almost scared. Oh, right, because he knows I'm touch-averse and gray-ace.

"I'm good."

"Really?" he nearly shouts, turning toward me.

"Yeah." I giggle, rotating back to him. The bed is a mess, we're both naked and deflated, but I'm still so at ease. How does this guy make me feel more comfortable in my skin than anyone ever has? "I really enjoyed that. Did you?"

"Hell yeah. I also haven't had sex in a while."

"Well, that wasn't *real* sex."

"Don't diminish what we just did, Sly."

"Okay, okay," I reply, putting my hands up. "I enjoyed the sexual activity we had, Omar. There."

"Better." His smirk fades as he looks at my lips. "Don't feel um…pressured to…We don't need to do it again if you don't want to."

"You're saying you'd want to?"

"Absolutely." He chuckles and it's adorable..

"You hook up with all sorts of guys and girls, so you probably don't have time…for me." What am I saying? Why am I trying to rebuff the advances of *literally* the one person on Earth I want to have sex with?

He laughs. "Sly, I just told you I haven't had sex in a while. I've been monastic this semester."

"Why?"

He shrugs. "I don't know. Busy with the play and soccer and stuff. But since you and I have similar rehearsal schedules…It might be convenient if you and I…

you know..." He looks so mischievous, and I wish I could say it wasn't making me horny. His hands are tied up, and yet somehow *he's* the one in control here? "It might help you get used to being touched on stage?"

Oh right, this is still all about the play. Of course —there's no romantic attachments when it comes to rolling around in bed with Omar, of all people. I don't know why a part of me thought he would actually like me that way. I bite my lip and look down. "What if I don't want to do much more? I'm still gray-ace, still new to all of this."

"That's totally fine, Sly. I had a lot of fun tonight, and even if that's all you wanna do, I'm down." He smiles, and I boil over and freeze at the same time.

I stare at him dubiously. "And you're okay helping me figure myself out?"

"Consider me your sexual tour guide."

"What?" I ask, giggling.

"You can ride this Alligator through the swampy waters of self-discovery." He sounds so melodramatic and we're both laughing now.

"Alright, alright." I stare at his perfect features wishing I could stay in his bed, wrapped in his arms forever. "I should go, though."

"One last thing, Sly?"

"Yeah?"

"Untie my hands. I need to pee."

17: Omar

"Enjoy the next two days off!" Aggie announces to the auditorium filled with students. "Because once we're back it's the fast track to 'dress rehearsal town,' and then our final destination 'opening night-ville!'" She claps, and everyone mutters, then disperses. I help a stage hand push away the rolling scenery in the shape of a boat, then walk back to gather my belongings.

"Mr. Odom," Aggie says, catching up with me. "Let's chat!"

"I was going to start posting the opening night flyers on my way out." I hoist up my backpack and wave the stack of yellow papers at her.

"It's not bad news. This will be quick. I'll walk with you." Most of the cast is out of earshot, so I feel okay with having a conversation right now. In the distance, I spot Sly, who gives me a subtle grin, then leaves the auditorium. It takes everything in me not to smile and wave back. "I just want to say I'm thoroughly impressed with the work you've done this semester."

"Thanks, Aggie." I stop and beam at her.

"You've been a real help. The musical is coming along, and most of it is thanks to you as my assistant director."

"Well, that's good to hear! Especially since I'm getting class credit for this."

"I know. I'm particularly impressed with the private directing sessions you've had with Mr. O'Rourke. Charles told me you spent lots of one-on-one time with him...going over...blocking."

She sounds like she's implying something, and I feel my face get warm. Halloween was a week ago, and we haven't been able to hook up again. Sly asked me to be discreet about it because, *duh*, his brother would never approve. Still, we're just having a little fun, and we've been totally professional during rehearsal. "Um..."

"Relax." Aggie smiles and bumps my elbow. "I would never address your private life if it was ruining the show. Clearly whatever you two have been doing is working. Sly and Charles are dynamite on stage now!"

I smile uncomfortably. "Uh...sure?"

"Anyway, I'm just glad to have you as my ward." We continue walking until we're out of the auditorium. "Have you considered pursuing drama after graduation?"

"What? I didn't know that was a thing."

"Oh, absolutely. I know you're an English major, but plenty of graduate programs in theater arts accept English bachelor degrees."

"But I'm not really an actor," I reply, eyebrows furrowed.

"There are other roles in the world of theater. I know of a few students of mine who have gone into the dramatic arts and now work on stage productions all over New York."

Wow. The idea of me getting to do this drama stuff on a professional level...It sounds fascinating. Is it possible I can make a career out of all this?

Aggie seems to see the conflict on my face. "Just think about it. Do your research. In any case, I've got a date with an older man. I'll talk to you later." She spins on her heel, her brown hair flipping backward. "Toodles!" Her shrill voice echoes down the halls of the Fine Arts building while I'm standing there, pondering my future.

I haven't gotten drunk in two weeks; this is a problem. The soccer team is doing well this season, but that just means more practices, games, and more finagling my schedule to wedge in play rehearsals. But tonight, me and the boys are free, so a party is calling my name. Kareem has been bugging me to go out, and I haven't seen my frat house buddies in a while, so I'm picking up Ravi and Steven to take them downtown.

After pulling up to the curb of their apartment complex, I text Ravi. He replies saying, "We're all on our way." Huh. That's a weird way to refer to him and Steven. Right when I think that, the back seat door opens, and I turn around.

"Look who's here!" I shout with a smile.

"Got room for me?" Landon asks. I'm thrilled

he's finally going out. Anything to get him out of his heartbroken slump.

"Hell yeah, we're gonna turn up. Wait, why aren't you in the front?"

"I respect the rules of 'shotgun.'" Landon shrugs while Ravi and Steven crawl in next to him. But if they're all back there then...

"Yeah, respect it." To my right, Sly has opened the passenger door. "I called it earlier. It's bro-rules, or road-rules, or something." He grins at me as he sits down, and he looks *good* too. He's got his glasses on and a dark green polo with a tight white thermal underneath. That, coupled with his black jeans, makes him look good enough to eat.

Bad Omar. No horny thoughts while Steven and Ravi are *literally* one foot away from you.

"It's okay that it's five of us, right, man?" Ravi asks.

I gulp and stare at Sly. The naughty look on his face makes it seem like he can read my mind. He must know how hot I am for him. "It's okay that I'm...*coming*, right?" he asks, his voice dripping in innuendo.

Alright, this gray-ace bastard is just toying with me now.

"Yup!" I squeak, putting my car in drive.

Fifteen minutes later, I pull up to the suburban house and the five of us hop out. The bass is booming as we walk in through the wooden door. "Omar!" A few of the guys I know cheer once we're in from the cold. They're all harmless frat bros who love me since I used to buy them liquor when they were only twenty. I point at each of them and greet them with a nod while the music blares through the walls. Some girls have appeared, flanking us on both sides while holding red cups. They're attractive too, throwing us 'do me' eyes. I'll never get over the power of being a soccer player at KU.

This is usually the part where I stake out and start planning on which girl, or sometimes guy, I want to take home. Not tonight, though; I'm acutely aware of that pretty boy standing right behind me. Had I known Sly was coming, I would have freshened up more and brought condoms!

We trail into the kitchen where the kegs are. I let Landon, Ravi, and Steven go ahead of me in line, and I hang back to where Sly is. Standing side by side, I give him a meaningful look. I want to ask him a million questions, and I know his brother can't hear us from here, but still, it seems risky.

"You seem nervous, Mr. Odom."

I glare at him. "I didn't know you were joining us tonight."

He shrugs. "I wanted to have a good time." He leans in closer. "Will you help me have a good time, Omar?" His whisper sends a chill through my body, and I shiver and step back.

"I uh...I gotta go!" I yelp, getting the attention of Ravi and Steven. Sly is, of course, smirking as I walk away. I'm down for us to hook up here in this frat house, but I don't wanna get caught by his brother or Ravi. So I should avoid Sly tonight, right?

18: Sly

This beer is terrible, and the music is too loud, which makes this a standard frat party. It actually isn't all that bad. My brother has been begging me to go out since I ditched him on Halloween. When I heard Omar was driving them to a frat party, I knew I had to capitalize on the moment.

Fooling around with Omar is going to have to wait; after chatting with Landon for a bit about his boy troubles, I'm finally back in a room with a fresh drink and ready to have a good time. Omar's here, along with Ravi, my brother, Kareem, his girlfriend Stacia, and a couple of others.

"Never have I ever...failed a class," Kareem says. There are a few murmurs and some people take sips.

"A D minus minus isn't failing, right?" Omar asks, and everyone laughs. "Alright, alright, who's next?"

I see the opening, and I take it. "I'll go!" I step forward and lift my cup in front of the circle of friends, garnering everyone's attention. "Never have I ever...given a blowjob to a guy." I stare at Omar who's looking back at me, his eyebrows flying up. There are hollers and cheers as, all around us, Landon, Ravi, and Steven all grin and take a sip. Kareem bumps his elbow into Omar and gives him a knowing glance, reminding him to take a sip.

After Omar's done drinking and the laughter dies down, I step back. I'm staring directly at Omar and smirking, feeling satisfied. I hope he now knows exactly what I want from him tonight. "It's your turn," I announce.

"Okay, okay," he says, shrugging. "Never have I ever..." A nefarious grin grows on his face, and he looks right at me. "Tied up my lover as part of a kinky sex act."

There are howls of laughter as people cheer and drink, and my face turns hot. I try to subtly take a sip of beer, but Landon points right at me. "Sly O'Rourke, you naughty boy!" he exclaims, getting everyone else to laugh.

The people around me are hollering and applauding, and I shrug, looking up like it's no big deal. These are my friends now, so it's all good. The old Sly would have been running for the hills at this point. "Well, things happen," I say.

"Ew, bro," Steven interjects. Oh yeah, my brother's here. "I don't think I can play this anymore with my brother here." Everyone is in hysterics, laughing at Steven's expense, and Ravi is patting him on the back, smiling. They start to move away when the bass starts up in another room.

"This is my jam!" Stacia says, dragging Kareem with her, and a few of the other girls are gasping and clapping. This effectively ends our little group drinking game, and everyone disperses out of the room.

Perfect, now's my chance. Omar's been looking delicious all night, and I want to make some more college memories, here and now.

Omar eyes me one last time before leaving the room, and I

follow him. I see him walk up the stairs, and I go the same route, making sure my brother isn't tailing me. Once I'm up there, I notice very few people wandering about, and Omar escapes into what I assume is the bathroom.

I stand in front of the closed door and take a deep breath. Hopefully the two watered-down beers give me the strength to do what I want tonight. The thought of kissing Omar and taking off his clothes again makes me dizzy with lustful anticipation. I have no idea how this aligns with me being gray-ace, but Wei said I should try to discover myself. I want to chase these feelings and see where they go; maybe I'll never feel this way about anyone again, so I need to make the most of my time with Omar.

The door opens, and I'm standing face-to-face with the man in question. *Here goes nothing.*

"Sly, I—" That's all he says before I gently push his perfect frame through the door. I turn around and shut it. Once I lock the knob, the tiny bathroom immediately gets hotter. "What are—"

"Omar." I turn around and stare at him, biting my lip. He looks me up and down, and I know I've got him. "I want... something from you." I lean close to him, and he walks backward until he's up against the wall. There's a tiny window behind him, a bathtub to my right, and a toilet and sink to my left.

"Wha...what's that?" he whispers.

"You promised to be my sexual tour guide," I purr, placing my hands on his chest. "I want to learn...so many things." My breath dances on his cheek and I drag my hands down slowly. I feel the lean muscle mass and flick the tiny nubs of his nipples through his shirt. His eyes roll, and a small moan escapes his lips.

"What do you...?"

"Tell me to stop, Alligator. Tell me to fuck off, that you're not down, and I'll leave." My hands go to the tips of his jeans, a few teasing fingers finding their way inside.

"I want to help you, Sly...I'll teach you just...tell me."

I lean even closer to his face, my lips a sliver away from his. "I want to know what it's like to taste your cock, Omar. Let me give you my first blowjob."

"Fuck," he whimpers, a part of him sounding like it just snapped in half. He aggressively catches my lips with his, and I'm back to the delicious taste of Omar's mouth. There's some stale beer mixed in, but his mouth on mine still makes me burn with lust.

If kissing was always like this, I probably would have come out as gay years ago. But no, it's just Omar. He's the only one who makes me want things. And right now, I hope he wants them too.

I pull back and look down between us, gripping his zipper. Nodding up at him, I ask, "May I?"

"Yes, *ohmygod*, Sly." He pushes my hands away, the impatient boy, and two seconds later, he gets his jeans and boxers down. Omar leans back on the windowsill, and I get on my knees. Last time, I didn't get a good look, but *damn* this is an impressive cock. He's hard, and he's bobbing just for me, waiting to be jerked or sucked.

"This will be my first time. My first lick of sex." I'm breathing on his dick, and Omar is staring down at me, mouth wide open. "Will you do me the honor?"

"I'll do whatever," he moans. "But are you sure you're comfortable? I know last time we did some bondage stuff."

"Just keep your hands behind your head, Alligator." He puts them up, and his shoulders and triceps bulge fantastically. "Perfect. Now let me know what you need me to do." I stroke that perfect rod of flesh, and his hips jut forward. "Do you want me to go slower"—I lick the tip—"or do you need more?"

"Need...more," he grunts. I notice him staring at the ceiling now, keeping his hands up. I chuckle to myself, victoriously. I've caught myself a hot jock by the cock.

Finally, I wet my lips and take him in. Little by little, I place his hard dick in my mouth. I'm a little uncomfortable, so I don't go all the way. I pull out, then take him back in and swallow more. I suck and lick, hoping it's a good technique; it's my first time, and I only know for certain to avoid teeth. Judging by the grunts and hip thrusts from above, I'm doing great work.

After a few minutes or so of jaw-aching sex, I hear Omar begin to breathe rapidly. "Sly...I'm gonna..." He's thrusting into my mouth, and I'm holding his dick by the base. Finally, he stops moving and shouts. The whole frat house may have heard him, but I don't fucking care. Omar Odom just came in my mouth, and it's everything I didn't know I wanted.

I swallow him down and keep sucking slower and slower until the spasms die down. After pulling off, I get some toilet paper and clean off his beautiful cock—I gotta treat it nicely if I want to play with it again!

Getting up, I notice him still leaning on the window sill. His eyes are shut and his mouth hangs open. "That...that was..." he croaks.

"Damn, I take it I did good for a first-timer?"

"You did fantastic, babe." He grabs my collar, leans in, and, with his eyes still closed, kisses me. I heard a lot of dudes don't like making out after receiving a BJ, but Omar doesn't care. The fact he called me *babe* is messing with my head.

I pull away and we grin at each other for a moment. "Hey um...do you want me to...?" He points at my crotch—so considerate of him!

"No thanks. That's too..." I don't want to sound like a coward, but the idea of him holding me down, even to blow me, scares me a little. I shiver. "No thanks. Don't need it."

"Okay," Omar replies, sounding worried.

"Another time, maybe?" I try to flash my sexiest grin. "Consider this a gift for you." I wink and wash my hands. "Hey, wait five minutes before walking out, yeah?"

"Of course," he says.

I leave the bathroom, and, fortunately, I don't see anyone around. The bass is booming when I head downstairs and rejoin the rest of the crowds. I swipe a cup of watered-down beer and exit the kitchen. Finally, I find my brother and Ravi listening to Kareem tell some soccer story. I stand next to them and pretend to listen as well.

"Hey." To my right, my brother is smiling at me. "How's your first time?"

"*What?*" I yelp.

"Your first frat party? How is it?"

I laugh in relief. Duh. "It's...great. Everything I've ever dreamed of." I sigh and smile, counting the minutes until I can see Omar again.

19: Omar

Being a senior in college is a mixed bag. It's crazy fun *and* super stressful. It feels like everyone's talking about grad school or entry-level business positions, but I'm trying to live in the now. Unfortunately, the now consists of multiple soccer games and practices, dress rehearsals for the play I'm helping direct, and trying to sort out my feelings for Sly.

I don't know how I got into this situation. It's a cliché story: hooking up with your best friend's boyfriend's little brother because he needed practice in the play you're directing since he's touch averse and asexual. See? *A tale as old as time!*

Except Sly likes having sex, at least sometimes. And he *really* likes it with me. Damn, for a gray-ace virgin, that dude's mouth is fantastic. But even if he wanted something more, relationships aren't for me. I still have the sour taste in my mouth of having feelings for *her*. On top of that, it's soccer-incest, bro-code violations, and all that. I just have to keep reminding myself of the reasons.

Soccer is a good distraction. My favorite game

with the guys I love more than anything in the world always tends to put me at ease. It's only really stressful when Coach chews us out for losing. This season, however, we've been on fire, losing only one preseason game and one actual season game. The KU Panthers haven't made it this far in years, and today we're getting on the bus having just won the semifinal.

"Let's go, boys! Finals, baby!" Kareem howls as he gets on the bus, and we all cheer.

"Whoop whoop!" Landon shouts from behind him.

"Alright, alright, settle down," Coach Dacks announces, finally getting on. "Let's get into it." We all take our seats and listen intently. "You've all been playing exceptionally well. I'm proud of you all, but we're not done yet. We're in the fight of your college careers in two days. Now's not the time to get cocky or complacent. Take tomorrow off and get some rest. We're meeting here at six a.m. sharp so we can hit the road to Maryland."

There are murmurs all around. "Go ahead," Coach Dacks adds, reluctantly. "You can celebrate...We're Division 2 regional finalists."

He plugs his ears and winces, and everyone shouts. "Eastern Regional Finals, *BABY!*" Kareem and Landon howl. Everyone's laughing and applauding as Coach sits down.

"In two days?" I ask Paul next to me. "So Friday I'll be away from campus?"

"Yeah." He looks puzzled. "Why? What's...Oh yeah, aren't you directing a play or something?"

I bite my lip and look down. "Yeah, something like that." Now that I'm not on the field, worry has set in. I'll be missing the opening night of the play, the project I put my heart and soul into for months. How's Aggie going to react? And, worse, what will Sly think?

"Oh, that's too bad," Aggie says. She puts her glasses on and looks down at her script. "But we'll just have to manage without you."

Seriously? "Um, okay. You're sure it's alright?"

"It is what it is. I always knew you had soccer commitments." She shrugs and walks over to the set design crew. "Hey, can we push the princess tower a smidge to the center after intermission?" she hollers. We've just finished our final dress rehearsal, and everyone's packing up. The cast performed flawlessly. I didn't even get peeved when Charles kissed Sly on stage. I was too distraught at the idea of missing opening night.

Sly walks up to me and is still wiping makeup from his brow. I guess he can read the disappointment on my face because he looks at me with concern. "Hey man, what's wrong?"

"I'm missing opening night," I moan, shoulders slumped. "For stupid soccer regional finals."

"I heard about that," he replies. "Doesn't sound stupid. According to Landee, this is the biggest game of the season."

"Who?"

"Landon. His first name is Landee."

"Oh." I shrug. He's my best friend but I'm just now discovering his first name. Go figure. "Yeah, but I wanted to be here," I whine. "I put so much of myself into *Izumi and Alex*. I wish I could do both." I sit down and frown at the floor.

"Aww...you'll be there at the next two shows! And the cast party on Sunday after the matinee? You're going, right?"

"Yeah." I look up at him, sitting next to me now, his hand on my back. "I'll be there."

"It's gonna be lit. We'll all get to relax, hang out. And who knows, maybe you'll come back as regional soccer champs? That'll be kick-ass."

"I suppose."

He looks down, then back up at me. "Hey, why don't we go get some frozen yogurt? Right now, my treat. You like froyo?"

"I have a tongue, don't I?"

"Oh, I *know* you do." He wags his eyebrows and I laugh. Even though I'm feeling down, Sly charms me. "Come on." He taps my shoulder, and we both stand up.

Fifteen minutes later, we manage to snag a far corner table at the Student Union Food Court. We've both got cups of froyo; mine's an orange cream with nuts and a cherry and his is a simple vanilla. We sit and eat in comfortable silence for two minutes before I realize what we're doing.

"This is nice," I say, intently watching him eat his dessert.

"Yeah, the froyo is so good here."

"No, I mean this." I point between the two of us with my spoon and he looks up. "Just us."

"What do you mean? We hang out all the time."

"Yeah, but for private play rehearsals or me being drunk or something." I scoop up some food to garner the courage to say more. "This feels like the first time we're...ya know... hanging, not banging."

Sly coughs up yogurt. I laugh as he grabs a napkin. "Sorry." I chuckle.

"No it's okay. It's just...I didn't even realize it."

"It's cool."

We eat quietly for a little longer. "So, about that frat party we went to..." I ask, staring at my cup. "And us...you know, hooking up." No one's within earshot, and from afar, hopefully we look like two friends hanging out.

"What?" Sly asks, his spoon dangling mid-bite. "Was I bad? Did I give a bad blow job?"

"No!" I laugh. He's way too adorable. "It's just...usually...I reciprocate. And I feel bad that I didn't."

"Don't be. I'm gray-ace, remember?"

"So you don't want it?" I manage to ask without sounding horny or desperate. I stare intently at the bottom of my cup, scraping up nonexistent yogurt.

"I mean, maybe someday. But like, sex never really mattered to me, and it still doesn't. The urge for me to want to have an orgasm...It comes and goes."

"Oh, okay."

"I still don't want to touch anyone or have anyone touch me most of the time. Though I did *thoroughly* enjoy having oral sex with you." His voice is deep and sexy, and I pull at my sweats to make room for my hardening cock.

"I uh...did, too." I feel a warmth on my cheeks. I've never blushed before. *What is this boy doing to me?* "If you ever want a repeat or want to try something else..."

"You'll be the first person I call." We grin at each other for a beat.

"Great. And thank you for all this." I tap my plastic spoon on my now empty cup.

"What?"

"Cheering me up. You didn't have to do that."

"Hey, you're like my best friend on campus! Anything for

you, Alligator."

I chuckle. *Friends.* Despite the cute nickname, I have to remind myself that's all we are.

"And I hope after the play is over, we'll remain buddies on campus!" He gets up to throw away his trash, and I'm sitting there stunned.

Oh shit. Once the play is over, I'll have no reason to hook up with Sly anymore. I knew this would happen but still. How am I supposed to remain friends with him when the thought of us not hooking up ever again makes me want to vomit frozen yogurt everywhere?

20: Sly

"Break a leg, Sly." That's it. Four words I got via text message from Omar thirty minutes ago. Steven told me they put away their phones before games, and this is the biggest soccer game in KU history. In fact, it seems like half the school joined my brother in taking a road trip down to Maryland to watch them. I'd feel bad about them all missing my play if I didn't have two more shows this weekend. Soccer is like a religion here, and even I recognize this as a huge event.

I'm sitting in the backstage area, twenty minutes until curtain call. Everyone else has opening night jitters, but I just keep re-reading Omar's text. Maybe there's a hidden meaning in those four words? He got really weird on me yesterday when I told him the play was ending. I know that implies we're not going to hook up anymore, but that's a good thing right? Omar Odom doesn't do strings, and I'm gray-asexual. He can have all the sex he wants, and he can just be my good friend on campus. It should be ideal, but why doesn't this feel like a win-win?

"Listen up, everyone!" Aggie's shrill voice cuts

116

through my inner turmoil, and I sit up straight. I'm clad in a green leotard with fake leaf trimmings, like some Peter-Pan-Jolly-Green-Giant hybrid. I'd say it's ridiculous, but the entire set of this musical is ornate and fantastical, so Dakin fits right in. "You've all done an extraordinary job! I'm so proud of the show that we've put together. You've all grasped what it means to be part of the dramatic arts, and I...I'm just..." She starts to tear up and waves her hands in front of her face.

There are some *awws* in our little crowd, so I say, "Omar texted me telling you to dry your tears, Aggie!"

This break up the tension and everyone laughs, including Professor Hark. "Yes, tell Omar to break a leg as well!" She raises a fist to cheer.

"I don't think we can say that to soccer players," I reply. Once again, everyone laughs, and we all disperse, getting ready for show time.

The first two acts go great, but now is the moment of truth. It's act three, the big love confession scene between Ezekiel and Dakin. My whole semester has been leading up to this. There are hundreds of people in the audience, but all that matters is what happens on stage.

Charles, dressed in a princely purple costume with a glittery cape, looks directly at me. "You are the most remarkable fairy gentlesir I've ever seen," he says, as Ezekiel.

"Have you seen many of my kind?"

"I don't need to. Dakin, you've done so much for me," Charles recites.

"It is you, Prince Ezekiel, who has saved me. You have allowed me to rediscover magic. I cannot thank you enough." I step forward and put my hand on Charles's face. "You make me believe again, Ezekiel. My feelings for you are so evident in this lush forest. 'Twas my magic, yes, but you were the spark that set my heart ablaze."

Here goes nothing.

Charles leans in, and I meet him halfway. I close my eyes, and my lips are on his. We've done this plenty of times in rehearsal, but the heat lamps of the stage are amplifying my discomfort. Hundreds of eyes are on me. I feel those anxiety butterflies make their way back down my spine.

I can't freak out now. There's an entire group song-and-dance number in like thirty seconds. *Focus on something, anything else to get you through this, Sly.*

Omar.

I hold the kiss and think of Omar—of his precious eyes, perfect stubble, and warm laugh. When I kiss him, it's actual magic. It's a blaze, it's lightning, it's a blizzard of emotions. Omar makes physical contact *feel right* to me.

We pull apart, and I smile as the orchestra plays the notes that signal for us to move off stage. Once there, Aggie whispers, "Great work, you two. Go go go!" She waves her arms like a windmill, and I move back to my place in line with the other actors.

Thirty minutes later, we all bow during the curtain call. Overall, the opening night of *Izumi and Alex* is a huge success. Even though he's not there, Omar is part of the reason I could get through it. I know it's been all about the play so far, but I need to face the truth; Omar Odom means something more to me. We have a connection, one I need to pursue, and I don't want to let him go.

21: Omar

Thousands of eyes are on us on the pitch. Fans on either side cheer or boo, but I can't listen to them right now. The team, *my* team, needs us to bring it home. The score is tied, and I refuse to let this go into extra time.

I sprint past their defenders, ready to take action should Ravi pass it to me. I huff and puff, mostly from nerves, because if we sink this, the title is ours. Landon is wide open, much closer to the goal, but I already know what Ravi wants to do. He doesn't need to say it; he's my best friend, and I can read his glances on and off the field.

He passes to me, but before I can get taken out by my opponents, I make a quick maneuver I've done a thousand times. Passing to Landon would be obvious, back to Ravi would be safe. But no one notices Paul, one of the shortest and fastest guys on our team.

Without even looking, I get the ball to him and he takes his shot. I can barely see the net, but the crowd cheers. The siren blares, and I look back to Coach Dacks roaring on the sidelines.

No freaking way—my assist may have just won

Korham University the men's soccer regional championship.

The next few minutes are a blur of cheering crowds and flashing lights. I hug so many of my teammates as we converge into a mass of sweat and brotherly love. We line up for so many pictures for our KU newspaper and local news outlets. Ravi wins MVP for putting in the most work this season, I think. I honestly can't tell; everyone's buzzing with joy. I've won so many soccer games over the years, but this is so much more. Having half the school come all the way to Maryland to see us take it all—no sports-related moment will beat this high, and I'm okay with that. Still, there is one final touch to this night that seems to be missing.

Once we're done showering, we walk out to see classmates, faculty, and family waiting to congratulate us outside the locker room. I high-five what feels like a hundred frat bros. A few girls take selfies with me and kiss me on the cheek, and I let them. Paul and Vince are loving the attention from the ladies, and even Landon seems to be enjoying himself. Before getting on the bus, I spot Ravi and Kareem hugging their respective significant others. Seeing the love they have makes me feel...I'm not sure.

"I'm jealous."

"What?" I nearly jump, hearing Landon behind me.

"I still want what Ravi has." He's staring at our friends as well, face filled with longing. "Not Steven, 'cause that's Ravi's guy but..." He shrugs and looks down. "I do miss having someone who gets me. A person I enjoy holding, who values me, ya know?"

I nod solemnly. I know Landon's still nursing that broken heart from over the summer.

"Sorry, you don't wanna hear this. You're Omar! You don't do strings attached. I probably sound lame to you." Landon gives me a self-deprecating chuckle.

"No, not lame at all," I mutter. I pat him on the shoulder, knowing I'm jealous, too.

Thousands of people cheered me on tonight, but I can't get my mind off of one person. I wanted to be there for opening night of the play, not just because it's my project, but because I wanted to see Sly fulfill his goal. *Izumi and Alex* is just as important to him, and to see him sing in front of the crowd would have been amazing. I know I'll be there tomorrow, but I've heard there's a certain theater magic to opening night and I'm disappointed I missed it.

But alas, I'm an athlete, and I have commitments. At least the season is over now.

Everyone's still full of life when we get on the bus. I finally turn on my phone, sift through some messages from my parents, and see one last text from Sly. "You're gonna do great, too. I couldn't have done this play without you this semester. See you later, Alligator."

I trace my finger up and down the text, reading it over and over. I wonder what it would have been like if Sly came to the game tonight. Maybe after my championship-winning assist, Sly would have run out onto the field and kissed me. The crowd would gasp or cheer, but I wouldn't care because I'd have the most amazing man in my arms.

That was the missing piece, the final touch that would have made this a perfect night.

22: Sly

"Man, we had an awesome run," Charles says. We're walking down the corridor in the Fine Arts building.

"We did. I had a blast!" I reply, wiping off some more makeup with the back of my hand.

"Me too."

"Hey guys!" Omar appears on my right, and I smile. He's been ever-present the past two shows, and we just finished our Sunday matinee. "What uh...what's up?"

"Just talking about how much fun we had." Charles looks between Omar and me like he wants to say something. Instead, he stops and points to his left. "This is me. Pleasure working with you, Omar. Sly, pleasure kissing you on stage."

I chuckle, and to my left, Omar has gone stone-faced. "Later, man," I say.

"Cast party tonight?" He points at both of us.

"Yeah. See you then!" With that, he's gone, and Omar and I walk toward where the audience has gathered.

It's silent for a beat before I say, "Hey, Omar, I

—"just as he says, "So, I've been thinking—"

We both awkwardly chuckle and look at each other. "That happens all the time in rom-coms," Omar says.

"People talking over each other? It really does. What did you wanna say?"

"You first."

"Well um..." I scratch my head. "You and I...just because the play is over doesn't mean we can't...ya know."

"Can't what?"

"Hang out and...and maybe we could keep hooking—"

"Uncle Sly!" Two little girls with bright red hair run up to us and land on either side of me.

"Hey!" I bend down to pat them on the heads. "How are my two favorite nieces?"

"We watched your play!" Lottie says.

"We saw you do magic on stage!" Lola adds.

"And you kissed a prince!"

"In front of everyone!"

"Aww, did you enjoy it?" I ask, bending down.

"Yeah!" they both chirp in unison. They can be manipulative with their six-year-old cuteness, but I have actually missed them since I've been to KU.

"They really did," my sister says, walking up to us. She's a superhero for working so hard and taking care of her twin girls all these years. "They loved the musical numbers. We all did." My parents are standing behind her.

"Hi Shannon. Mom. Dad." That's when I remember Omar is still next to me. "Um, family, this is ... Omar."

"You're the director!" Shannon says.

"Assistant director." He smiles and blushes,

looking at his shoes.

"And he helped win the soccer championships with Ravi," I add. He rolls his eyes and shrugs. I swear he continues to get more adorable.

"Wow! A performing artist and an athlete!" Mom says, pointing at me, then Omar. Now it's my turn to blush. "Has a certain ring to it."

"Thank you, Mrs. O'Rourke."

"Um, sure," I add. "Anyway, you all probably have to hit the road right?"

"Already?" the twins whine.

"Yup. But I'll see you at Thanksgiving!"

"What about you?" Shannon asks Omar. "Do you have any plans for Thanksgiving? We're already hosting Ravi, and there is plenty of room."

"Uhh…" Omar stares at me, and I try to keep my expression neutral. "My family usually does lunch."

"Oh well, that's too bad!" I reply.

"But we do dinner! Want to come by? Any friend of Sly's is a friend of ours!" Mom says.

Omar looks at me with his kind eyes. "I think I live about an hour away from you, but I get so bored on Thanksgiving night. I'd love to make the trip." He smiles down at the girls. "You ladies want me to bring pumpkin pie?"

"Yeah!" They both squeal, and everyone laughs.

"Then it's settled! We've got to make the long drive back now, but we'll let you boys go," Shannon says.

"We really *really* hope to see you at Thanksgiving!" Mom says, patting Omar on the arm.

Once they're gone, I quickly mutter to Omar that I need to change and disappear. The prospect of him being in my house, around my family, makes me nervous for some reason.

The Italian restaurant Marino's has been converted into an open layout tonight for the cast party of *Izumi and Alex.* The lights are dim and all thirty of us cast and crew have made it. There are three open salad bar tables and everyone is milling around, mingling, eating, and generally enjoying themselves. I'm in a dark corner sipping on a margarita.

Omar is across the room talking to Aggie and her date, an older guy wearing a plaid shirt. I'm trying to sort out my feelings for him before he comes to my house on Thanksgiving, the same house where I share a room with my brother. Ravi will probably be sleeping over again. Last year, the idea of seeing Steven and Ravi flirting all night made me want to puke, and while that hasn't changed, I'm definitely more comfortable with the concept of intimacy.

I wonder if Omar will want to be intimate with me again. Or is he done with me now that the play is over? Shit, do I want us to be done? Of course not. He's the first person, guy or girl, to make me feel alive. He makes me smile and laugh, and when we're intimate, the world finally makes sense for once.

I was cold and lonely, and Omar was a flash flame that engulfed my body; I never want him to stop keeping me warm.

But why would he bother to continue hooking up with a gray-ace guy like me? Omar is outgoing and fun and loves sex. He deserves a partner that actually suits him. I could never be the kind of person he'd want to date—that's assuming he'd ever want to be locked down by anyone!

Stupid, Sly. How could I let myself catch feelings for someone so unavailable?

"Sup," Charles slides up to me, drink in hand, and puts his arm around me. I squirm, and he immediately drops it. "Oh, sorry, I forgot."

"No worries." I shake out any nerves and get back to standing next to him, inches apart.

"I know you don't like being touched, so, my bad."

"How did you know that?"

"Please. We had to basically make out multiple times the past month. I've gotten more action from you than any girl this semester, which is *so* sad."

"Oh, right." I shrug and look down. I always got straight vibes from him, but I don't like to label people in my head.

We stand in silence for a few seconds more. "I'm kinda glad this is over, ya know?"

"Why is that? So you don't have to kiss me anymore?" I smirk at him.

"No. Well, yes, but not because of that. I don't care about kissing you. It doesn't make me gay. I only auditioned because the girl I liked was auditioning. But what concerns me..." He points with the drink in his hand, and I follow with my eyes. Omar is glaring at us from across the crowded restaurant.

"What?"

"Whenever I'm on stage with you, Odom looks like he wants to throw a dagger at me."

I nearly spit up my drink.

Charles chuckles. "Omar always looks like he wants to kill me. Every. Single. Time we're together."

I shake my head. "He's doing it right now," he whispers. I look over to see Omar is, in fact, closely watching us. His jaw is clenched, and he looks like he's ready to start a fight. He has never once shown an ounce of aggression at me, which means he really dislikes Charles.

"What did you do to him?"

Charles laughs. "I committed the sin of being cast as your love interest. Your boyfriend is mad possessive, yo."

I feel my face prickle. "He's...not my boyfriend."

"Ah." He takes another sip. "Well, do everyone a favor and work out whatever it is you two are doing. I'm going to go drink more to gain the courage to ask out Celia. And walk away from *you* before Odom decides to throw a soccer ball at my face or something."

We both giggle, and he leaves. Right on schedule, Omar strides up to me.

"Everything alright?"

"I'm good."

"Was Charles bothering you?"

"No." I can't help the little grin that grows while I drink my margarita. No one's ever been jealous over me before—I kinda love it.

"You two aren't...?" He looks so serious.

"No! We're just castmates. I don't want anyone to touch me, remember?"

"Right." He smiles, looking relieved.

"Except *some* people." I wink.

Omar chuckles. "You sure you're okay with me coming to Thanksgiving dinner?"

"Are *you* okay with it? You'll have to play with my cousins and the twins, and they're not easy to manage."

"Beats being at my house." He shrugs, and I finish my margarita.

"Well, great. Then I guess I'll see you at O'Rourke headquarters, my friend." I reach out to shake his hand. His face falls flat, and he pauses for a moment, then he smiles again and shakes my hand.

"Can't wait, Sylvester." Neither can I.

"When you said you invited a friend from the play, I thought you meant, like, Tisha. I didn't think it would be Omar." Steven and I are putting down placemats for the kids' table in our parents' living room. The number of kid table settings has certainly grown over the past seven years.

"Why not? Omar *is* my friend." I put down more pink paper cups. My face is getting warm and I shift my glasses up my nose. "He's like the best friend I've made at this school. You invited *Ravi*."

"Yeah, but that's different," Steven retorts. He picks up some stray toys from the floor. "Ravi and I are boning. You and Omar are not."

"Ew." I squirm dramatically. "Please, I don't

wanna hear about that."

Steven sniggers. "I'm just saying...Omar has a *reputation*."

Now I'm starting to get mad. "We're just friends. And besides, *Mom* invited him."

Steven stares at me like he doesn't believe anything I'm saying. "Just...be careful, Sly."

Before I can lash out at my brother, I hear the doorbell. I stride up to the front door, fix my tie underneath my black sweater vest, pat down my hair, then open it.

Omar Odom is at my house, dressed in a red two-piece suit, and he looks more delicious than the pumpkin pie he's holding. This holiday just got better, and now I *really* have something to be thankful for.

His eyes look dull, though, like something's weighing on his mind.

"Hey!" I beam at him. "You made it!"

He quickly pulls himself together and plasters on a fake smile. "Yeah! Happy Thanksgiving!"

"Same to you. Are you alright?"

"Yeah! Totally! Where are the little ones?"

Just then, the twins run up to us from around the corner of the house where they were playing. Ravi is trailing not far behind them. "You brought pie!" they squeal in unison.

"I sure did!"

"What do we say to Omar?" I ask.

"Thank you, Uncle Omar!" They're too cute.

"Aww, you little ladies can call me Uncle Alligator!"

The twins giggle, and I feel something spark in my heart. I can see the girls calling him that for years to come, but I don't think Omar will ever settle down, least of all with me. Still, a guy can dream.

"Let's go play hopscotch!" Lottie chirps.

"Yeah, let's go!" Lola adds.

"Uh, I have to take this pie inside first."

"No! I'll handle the pie." Ravi cuts in and grabs it. "You go play hopscotch!" He leans into whisper, "I'm exhausted already!"

"Yay!" the twins cheer in unison. The girls grab Omar's hands and pull him back out the door.

"Hey, you were the MVP, Mr. Soccer captain!" Omar yells while being dragged away.

"Can't hear you!" Ravi sings while walking into the living room.

Thanksgiving is a blast, and Omar fits in perfectly with my family. The twins and my cousins all love playing hopscotch with him, and he helps them create artistic masterpieces with sidewalk chalk on the gravel. I spend a chunk of the evening sipping a drink and smiling fondly while Omar tries to keep up with all their little games. I can tell my parents think he's charming whenever they engage him in conversation. Steven keeps giving me weird looks, but he's distracted by Ravi feeding him food or smiling —really, anything Ravi does has Steven throwing heart eyes.

I try to ignore that nagging feeling telling me Omar should be a permanent fixture by my side at every family holiday from now on. A future with him is a pipe dream, and just entertaining the idea is a slippery slope to heartbreak.

It's dark out when I finally walk Omar to his car.

He parked down the block, and no one from my family is around, so it's nice to get this modicum of privacy with him.

"This afternoon when you came by, you seemed...I don't know, off." I lean against his car door, and Omar joins me, looking up.

"Yeah well...my Bangladeshi family's Thanksgiving lunch was worse than usual this year."

"What happened?"

He sighs at the night sky. "I shouldn't even be telling you this. It's my baggage. You don't wanna hear it."

"I do." *Because I care about you, you beautiful bastard.* "Because...we're friends. Plus, I'm a problem-solver kind of guy. That's why I'm majoring in Sociology at KU. I want to be a social worker."

Omar looks at me, an expression of, dare I say, fondness in his eyes. For a few moments, all we hear is the chirping of bugs on this warm November night.

"You're going to make a great social worker one day." He buzzes his lips and looks up again, seeming defeated. "That's the problem," he continues. "You're driven, and I'm not."

"What do you mean?"

"During lunch, my dad called me out on not knowing what I want to do with the rest of my life. And honestly? Facts. I *don't* know what I'm doing."

"Well, what do you enjoy doing? Soccer?"

He scoffs. "Look, I love soccer, but it's just for fun. I'm nowhere near good enough, and the life of a pro athlete is *not* one for me. I only joined the KU soccer team because...Well, it doesn't matter. I don't have a future in that."

Huh. I wonder why he joined. Instead I ask, "Okay, then what drives you?"

"I'm an English major. But the only class I really enjoyed was the independent study in theater arts." He stares right at me, stars shining in his brown eyes. "Being with you and the rest of the cast made me feel alive for the first time ever."

"I think I know the feeling." I want to tell him that kissing him makes me feel alive for the first time, too. But I say nothing.

"But there's no career in that."

"Why not?"

"Huh?"

"Omar, you were *so* good at directing and producing. I'm sure Aggie would love for you to be her assistant next semester for the spring show. And we live in New York. There are theaters all over the state. You could explore that!"

"You really think so?"

"I don't see why not. I'll even help you compile resources, like internships and drama schools. Steven is going into art education. I'm sure together, you and I can find a graduate program like he did to hone your skills and make professional connections. I'll help you!"

A slow smile grows on Omar's face. "Alright. That sounds great!"

"We'll work on it...Together."

"Thanks. You don't have to do this. Why are you helping me?"

My pulse races. "*Just tell him you want him, all of him, for real,*" the voice inside my head says. "Because...like I said, we're friends." I beam at him and put my hand out for him to shake.

He hesitates, then shakes it as well. "Right. Goodnight,

Sly." He opens the car door and I step aside.

"See you later, Alligator."

He smiles, then looks down, not moving. When his eyes meet mine again, they're filled with another emotion. It's desire, but mixed with something more. I don't know what it is or why I do what I do next.

I find myself crowding his space, pulling on his jacket, and putting my mouth on his. He puts his hand on my cheek and kisses me back slowly. Omar's touch is an inferno in my soul, and I never want to put it out. His kiss is sweet and burning like always, but this time it's also tender and quiet. We're not in a rush. We're not trying to get off. It's just me, Omar, and the night sky.

When I finally pull back, reality sets in. "S-sorry," I stammer. "I forgot...the play is over. We don't need to practice. And we're not...I'm sorry." I spin on my heel and walk back briskly to the house, not wanting to look at his face or hear him reject me.

Get it together, Sly. Guys like Omar don't end up with ace dudes. That's just not how life works.

23: Omar

"Let's give it up for the regional champions, the women's swim team!" There's a round of applause and cheers inside the Athletics Center, now decked out in dazzling Christmas decorations. "And your regional champions, the men's soccer team!" When Logan says this, our table erupts, with me cheering louder than anyone. "We want to thank all the teams for another great semester and another awesome year! Happy holidays, and enjoy!"

The music starts to play again, and everyone goes back to chatting and eating. I'm at the annual Athletics Formal, dressed to the nines, and I'm seated at a table with my favorite people in the world, my soccer boys. In keeping with tradition, I opted not to take a date. Paul, Vince, and Kareem all have pretty ladies on their arm, and Steven is of course here with Ravi.

I refuse to admit I'm lonely because that would imply I want affection, which is dangerously close to romance. Landon is also date-less. He's seated next to me grinning at his phone, so he's no fun to talk to right now. Off in the distance, I spot Logan kissing Wei, who's been intermittently performing with the music department tonight.

Wei points to the conductor, and a slower melody starts to play. Ravi taps on Kareem's shoulder, and soon, they're dragging Steven and Stacia out onto the dance floor. Just like a year ago, my soccer boys start the first slow dance of the night, inspiring plenty of other couples to join in.

Ravi is gazing so intently at Steven, as if they haven't been dating for over a year and don't sleep together every night. This naturally reminds me of the other O'Rourke brother, the one who's been plaguing my every thought.

The logical side of my brain believed Sly and I were through after the play was over. It wasn't a relationship, just some mild experimentation. But that part of my brain tends to shut off whenever I'm around Sly. The truth is, I want to date him for real. People have tried to get me to care about relationships for the past four years, and along comes this beautiful asexual dude who gets under my skin. He makes me forget the reasons I don't believe in romance and makes me want to settle down with him. Sly O'Rourke is thoughtful, courageous, and comforting; life is better when he's with me.

Now I'm sitting here eating cocktail wieners, ruminating over that scorching hot kiss from two weeks ago. I haven't spoken to him since Thanksgiving. With finals slamming everyone and no play rehearsal, I've only had time to text him little greetings. Shit, what else would I even say?

Hey, Sly, I know I'm a commitment-phobe, and I know you don't like being touched, but do you maybe want to date? I'm sure that would go over well.

Even more couples join in on the dance floor, and I spy Ravi leaning in to gently kiss Steven. Okay, *nope*, I'm done. I head upstairs, hopping up the bleachers to get above ground and leave. I need some air.

I sit down at a bench right outside the Athletics Center. It's chilly out, but my white suit keeps me warm enough. I look up at the stars, trying to get rid of these stupid feelings. Omar Odom doesn't *do crushes* or relationships. I learned a long time ago they hurt too much. Besides, Sly deserves someone better, someone who can actually do the relationship thing without hesitation.

"Is this seat taken?" I hear Landon approaching but I don't even bother tilting my head.

"It's a free country. Or free bench. Or not really free, tuition is kinda high." I gaze at my foggy breath as it dissipates above me in the cold.

After a few seconds, Landon breaks the silence. "Is now a good time to say that Dane and I got back together?"

"No way!" I bring my head forward and grin.

"Yup," he says, a smile growing on his face. "He came to my house over Thanksgiving break. He'll be back next semester, but we talked it over, and we're starting our relationship again."

"That's amazing!" I knew Dane was returning from his sabbatical in January and that Landon was gonna fight to get his man back. Glad to hear they've patched things up sooner. "Congrats, bro."

"Thanks." We pound fists, and I go back to staring down at nothing. "A year ago, seeing all that lovey-dovey crap on the dancefloor made me so jealous."

"Mm," I reply.

"I didn't think you *did* jealousy."

"I don't."

"Why didn't you just *ask* Sly to come with you as your date?"

"Because we're not dating." *Shit.* "Wait, how did you know?"

"I didn't. You just confirmed it." My face feels warm and I want to smack the smug grin off his stupid, symmetrical face. "Actually, it was because of that frat party we all went to."

"What do you mean?" I wipe my hands on my pants as my pulse races.

"I saw you guys coming out of the upstairs bathroom like two minutes apart."

"I knew I should've waited longer," I mutter.

"Relax," Landon chuckles. "I didn't tell anyone. Your private life is *your* business, bro. I just hope you're not like...hurting him."

"I'm not!" I sit up straight, then clear my throat. "I honestly have no idea what we're doing."

"Look, if Dane was here, I'd be slow dancing with him right now. You have that opportunity."

I pause and look at my hands. "Dealing with real feelings is scary. I was too chicken-shit to ask Sly to the formal."

"He's at the apartment right now, alone. Probably reading on the couch or something. What are you waiting here for?"

"I don't know…" I shrug. Is it possible Sly is willing to see me? If this were a movie, I could barge in with a grand romantic gesture. Sly loves romantic movies.

"As Dane's friend once said, 'Go. Get. Your. Boy.'"

He pokes my shoulder with each word, and I grin.

"Thanks, bro." I get up and run to my car.

I knock on the door of the second-floor apartment. I catch my breath and smooth my hair. I noticed on the drive up here the living room light is on. According to Landon, Sly likes to read in the common area. I really hope my plan works.

The door opens, and Sly looks equal parts confused and concerned. He's got his glasses on, a graphic T-shirt, and gray sweats. He looks positively comfy. "Omar?"

"Can I come in?"

"Sure." I walk in and steel myself to finally tell him the truth. "Why aren't you at the formal? Is something wrong?"

"Well...no, but yes." I pace back and forth through the living room.

"You're scaring me, man. Did something happen?"

"What happened was...I saw your brother. Slow dancing with my best friend, Ravi."

"Okay?" Sly asks, rightfully puzzled.

"And I wanted to dance for the first time in my life, but I couldn't. I guess...the reason I came here is because...this is what the heroes do...in those cheesy movies." I bite my lip and close my eyes.

"Huh?"

I take another deep breath, in and out. I put my phone down on the side table next to Sly's book. To do this right, I stream the song "Find Me" by Boyce Avenue as loud as I can. I click off one of the two lamps so the room is darker. The slow strumming of the guitar mixed with the mood lighting make the whole living room look perfect.

"What are you doing?"

"Sly, I want *this* to be our rom-com. I came here because…dancing with anyone else doesn't feel right. I don't want to hook up with anyone else, and I don't want us to stop seeing each other just because the play is over. I want *you.*"

His eyes look glossy, even in the semi-darkness. "What are you saying?" he asks, his voice barely above a whisper.

I hold out my left hand and smile. "I suppose… I'm asking you to slow dance?"

I guess I said the right thing, a moment later, Sly puts his right hand in mine and moves closer to me. He places his left hand on my shoulder, and I gently put a hand on his hip. "Is this okay?" I ask.

"With you, always." He places his head on my shoulder.

We sway for a moment to the romantic music, and it's everything I've ever dreamed of and more. Sly O'Rourke has brought back to life that seedling of hope I thought died years ago. "I really like you, Sylvester."

"I like you too, Alligator. But I'm still gray-ace. I could never give you all the sex you want. Then next year, you'll have graduated and I'll still be here. Not to mention my brother and Ravi will never accept us together. They'll say it's against bro-code, and then—"

"Shh…" I say, patting his head. "I know, just… dance with me for now, okay?"

"Okay." We sway and enjoy the next two minutes of music. I wanted him at the Athletics Formal, but at least I have him now. I thank my lucky stars I get to share this moment with this man.

"This is really corny," Sly says.

"I know." Soon, we're both laughing while still entangled in each other's arms.

He pulls back, looking at me, then gently kisses me. "But it's perfect. Just like the movies."

My smile grows wider. "Better than the movies."

24: Sly

I lie on my bed in my apartment room and scroll through the last few texts I got. They're all from Omar saying mundane stuff like "Happy New Year to you as well" and "I'll be back on campus that day, too. Let's hang out." So he wants to see me, but does that mean he still likes me? What else does it mean to "hang out"? Omar had to leave the dorms a few days after the Athletics Formal, and I haven't seen him since. Before he left, he told me he wanted us to pick up where we left off this coming semester—does that mean we're dating? I agreed because it seemed so pragmatic at the time. But now? I just want to know what our label is.

Relationships are hard, and putting your heart on the line is scary. No wonder Omar and I avoided them all these years!

Still, I have this inkling Omar has a rough past with relationships. I need to ask him about it sometime. He implied he was on campus already, and my brother, Ravi, and Landon won't be back until tomorrow, which is convenient. Do I ask him out on a date? Or is that too lame? Will I need to put out if we *do* go on a date?

I groan and put my pillow on my face. Overthinking really is my MO.

I take off the pillow and dial up the only person I can talk to.

"Hello?"

"Hey, Wei. how are you?"

"Hey, Sly. I'm well."

"How was your break?"

"The holidays were good. Spent Christmas with my family. Logan kind of went overboard with buying gifts for everyone. It's his first Christmas with other people in like, six years."

"Aww…" I sit up and clear my throat. "That sounds sweet."

"It was. Did you need something?"

"Can we have an impromptu Safe Space chat?"

"Of course! Sly, I consider us friends. You can talk to me about anything."

"Okay." I close my eyes and put my fingers on my eyelids. "Right before winter break…me and this guy…we slow danced. And kissed."

"That sounds nice."

"No, it's lame. Other people my age are having sex."

"Sly, I told you. Go at your own pace. Don't do anything you're not comfortable with."

"Right…anyway, we're back on campus, and I don't know if we're picking up where we left off or not."

"What did he say when you asked him about your relationship?"

I cringe and I guess Wei can hear it over the phone. "Sly…

144

you *did* ask him about where your relationship stands, right?"

I sigh. "No, not yet."

"Sly! Come on! You're second-guessing everything, aren't you?"

"Yes, because that's what I do!" I whine and put on my glasses and start pacing around the room.

"Sly, in my relationship experience, it's best to just tell the other person you like them and want to be with them. In a romantic sense. No bullshit, just be clear."

"Ugh, that makes me sound so virginal."

"Aren't you...?"

"Yes. I'm virginal and inexperienced and just lame!" I whine.

"Well, doesn't this guy know you're a virgin?"

"Mm...yes."

"And didn't he like you enough to slow dance and kiss you?"

"Yes?"

"Does this special person of yours seem like he'll reject you for any of those things you just said?"

"No," I reply. "He's understanding, and caring...and warm...and sweet." I swoon over the phone.

"Then you need to establish real communication with him."

I sigh. "Okay. I'll go be mature and ask him what's going on in his head."

"Good man."

"And Wei? Thanks for listening to me be a dumbass."

"It's cool. Talking about your feelings with your crush is never easy, even when you're in your thirties." Wei chuckles. "Talk to you later."

We say our goodbyes and hang up. I bite my lip, look down and flick to Omar's number, which is in my phone under 'Alligator.'

Before I can overthink even further, I click 'dial.'

"Hey you," he says on the second ring. Just the sound of his voice gets my blood pumping, but I still don't think I'm in the mood for sex.

"Omar, hey! How was your, um, break?" I wince at my stuttering voice.

"It was good. Kinda boring. I texted you for most of it." I force a laugh, and he continues, "But I've been having a tough time trying to find nearby theater arts graduate programs, especially ones that will accept me on shorter notice."

"I can help you with that! Two heads are better than one, and all that...crap." I cringe again at my corny lines. "How about you come over?"

"Tonight?" I can tell he's smiling over the phone.

"Yeah. Steven, Ravi, and Landon aren't back yet."

"Oh, so you're all alone," he replies, sounding intrigued.

"We can do research...together."

"I suppose I can come by if you answer one question."

I gulp. "What's that?"

"Do you prefer tofu or shrimp pad thai?"

* * *

An hour later—and three outfit changes until I settled on a tight gray long-sleeve Henley that I think hugs my chest *just* right—there's a knock on my door. Opening up, I see the only person, guy or girl, I've ever been attracted to holding a plastic bag of food. He's grinning and is wearing a large black coat and a green winter cap with a bobble on it. It's been awhile, so his hair is slightly longer and he's got some expertly styled facial hair. In short, he's gorgeous, and I really hope I can make him mine.

"Something delicious is at your door!" he announces. "And I brought food, too." He winks and I giggle. "Sup, O'Rourke?"

"I'm good! You can just put the food down in here on the um...coffee table."

He follows me into the living area where I've got my laptop on the couch. "So I've been looking up some programs. There are a few in New York and New Jersey with spring deadlines, actually."

I hear him set the food down, but notice out of my periphery that he's just standing there looking at me. He says nothing, so I continue, staring at my screen. "I know some accept English majors, but some want a bachelor's in theater arts, which I didn't know was a thing." My voice trails off, and I adjust my glasses. He's still not moving or saying anything, and it's killing me.

"There are also a few that are further upstate, like...like five hours away. I'm surprised how many there actually are. Some degrees you can bang out in one year and get that bachelor's and...and..."

"Sly," he says. I still refuse to look at him, opting instead to babble on.

"There are some famous Broadway directors who have graduated from these programs, so...so...that's awesome for you and..."

"Sly!" he repeats, louder now, and it startles me. I look up to see a smug grin on his face. "Can you please get over here?"

"Uh, okay." I stand up and adjust my glasses. My face is on fire as I step closer to him. *It is really warm in this apartment.* I need to check the thermostat. "How did you want to look them up? I can organize them by tuition...or...or distance."

"That's all fine and dandy," Omar says, quirking an eyebrow. "But I was hoping we could discuss picking up where we left off in December?" He grins, and I swear my pulse doubles.

I shrug and look anywhere but at him. "Okay... Well we were researching your career options, so we could definitely work on that or...talk about this semester's theater options. I heard Aggie is doing another school musical, so that would be great for your résumé and uh..."

Omar gives the biggest eye roll in the history of facial expressions. "Sylvester O'Rourke, am I going to have to shut you up with a kiss like in the movies? I know how much you hate nonconsensual surprise touches."

I gasp and nod. He slowly leans in and places his mouth on mine, and, just like in a rom-com, I melt. I absolutely fold in Omar Odom's arms, moaning the entire way. I've missed him so damn much, and kissing him feels like coming home.

25: Omar

Much to our credit, we stop making out eventually and *do* actually get some research done for theater arts programs. We eat our dinner, and by the end of the evening, Sly has finished typing up the list of relevant colleges and application websites, all for me. My man is so smart and helpful.

That's right. I want to make Sly my man.

Once we've saved our list, I stand up and make a dramatic yawn. "Whew, it's getting pretty late."

"Yeah, I don't want to keep you too long. I know pre-season practices start tomorrow," Sly says.

"Please, the spring season barely counts for anything. Especially now when you're talking to the regional champions." I flex my biceps with a cocky grin. I don't miss the heat that flares in Sly's eyes when he looks at my arm.

I straighten my shoulders again and relax my face. "Thanks for everything tonight," I say, opting for a serious tone.

"No problem." He clears his throat, and we

stand there in awkward silence. "Let me...walk you out?"

Here goes nothing. "Or I can stay the night?" I ask, looking up as if it's no big deal.

"Huh?"

"Steven's not here to nag at us. Can I stay overnight?"

I look down to see him squirming and readjusting the buttons on his shirt. "I don't...I'm not really..."

"What's wrong?"

"I just...I still don't *want to* have sex, Omar," he blurts, eyes screwed shut.

Oh, is that it?

"Wait, what?" I ask, and his eyes open. "I didn't say I wanted to have sex."

"But...but...you asked to stay overnight."

"Yeah, because I wanted to cuddle with you." I walk closer to him and, in a bold move, put my hands on his hips, pulling him in. He's not shuddering, so I take it as a good sign. "I missed you like crazy over break. I wanted to catch up, to stay up talking and get to know the *real* Sly. Then, I could wake up in your arms. I think that'd be romantic and delightful. Because *you're* delightful."

His face reddens. "But I'm gray-asexual. Wouldn't you rather be with someone who's not like, broken?"

"You're not broken," I reply immediately. "There's nothing about you I need to fix."

"Really? You're not expecting me to––"

"Babe, I'm not gonna force you to do anything you don't wanna do. That's not what boyfriends do."

"Boyfriends?" he yelps, going stiff in my arms.

"Well, yeah. I told you I wanted to be with you

before Christmas. I thought this was us picking up where we left off?" Shit, did I get this wrong?

"I didn't...didn't realize. I've never had a girlfriend or boyfriend."

"Funny that," I whisper, smiling. I lean in and caress his cheek. "I've never had a relationship either. Guess we're learning about this together." Finally, he meets me halfway, bridging the space between our mouths. It's a sweet, slow kiss that has me moaning seconds later.

When we finally pull apart for air, he has a glossy look on his face. "You drive me crazy, Sylvester."

He chuckles. "Would you like to spend the night in my arms?"

"Really? You're okay with it?"

"If you're okay with not having sex with your boyfriend."

Hearing him declare himself my boyfriend has me shivering in the best way. "Is cuddling allowed?"

He beams at me and pecks me on the lips. "Let's go get washed up, Alligator."

We don't end up showering together, which is a shame. Still, despite his hang-ups and mine, Sylvester O'Rourke wants to be my boyfriend, and with him in my arms, I feel indestructible.

Once we're done brushing our teeth, it's almost midnight and he's sitting on his bed in pajama pants and a white T-shirt. "Is it alright if I just wear my boxers to bed?"

"Fuck yeah," he whispers, staring at me. He coughs and says, "Um...yes, that's fine."

I smile internally and make a very long show of

taking my shirt and pants off. A few seconds later, I'm crawling into bed with him and he's shutting off the lights. He curls up on my chest, and for the first time in weeks, I feel complete.

All those months of watching him act on stage and not being able to hold him the way I wanted have led to this. I might be graduating this May, but I'm going to make every moment I have with Sly count.

"So, you wanted to get to know me, right?" Sly asks.

"I heard learning about your boyfriend is an important part of a relationship. Allegedly. Again, I've never done this before."

He giggles against my chest and it makes my heart flutter. "Ask me anything."

"Is your brother gonna kill me when he finds out?"

"No." He laughs. "Though I *am* kind of dreading that conversation. He's so judgy sometimes...like, I just don't understand how you and I dating is any of his business."

"It's my fault." I sift my fingers through his brown, trimmed hair. "I have a reputation for getting around. Probably because...I used to get around."

"So I've heard, but I don't care. And I don't care if Steven tells me to stop. I'm not gonna stop seeing you."

Hearing this makes me want to shatter into a cascade of fireworks. Sex is nice, but hearing this gorgeous man say he's invested in our relationship feels way better. "Alright, your turn."

"Hm?"

"Ask me something you wanna know about me," I say.

Sly shifts in bed so he's lying next to me. He stares at me, and I count the few freckles on his face while the moonlight shines on him. "The day we met...you told me romance doesn't exist for people like you."

"I said that?" I ask, shifting over so I'm lying on my right side.

"Yeah. You were really drunk, but I never forgot it. It was like you were lamenting how romance wasn't meant for you. Then I found out you don't do relationships, but you read romance books, and like...all the clues kept adding up. It's kind of why I thought you didn't want to be with me initially."

I look down, not wanting to see his beautiful brown eyes. My pulse is pounding because I know I'm about to tell him the truth. My hand has found its way to his and I lace our fingers together.

"I do want to be with you, Sly. I know that. But I had a shitty thing happen to me when I was in high school. It made me never want to have a girlfriend or a boyfriend." I gulp down and try to summon the courage to continue.

"Hey, you don't have to tell me," Sly whispers. He holds my hand tighter. "It's your story. You are entitled to your privacy."

"It's okay." I lie back and stare at the ceiling, then take a deep breath. "I've always loved the idea of romance, even as a kid. I devoured young-adult romance fiction. So, when I was a senior in high school, I took an advanced English literature class. There was a new gorgeous English teacher on the block; let's call her Juliet."

"Okay," Sly replies, tracing his hand up and down my arm.

"She was super young, only twenty-six at the

time. She looked like Cameron Diaz, and all the dudes at my school had a crush on her; I was no exception. I did well in her class, told her I wanted to major in literature, which was true, so we had afterschool sessions where we would work on my essays. We spent hours talking about our favorite novels, authors, and characters. She helped me get into an English lit college program."

"That sounds...nice?" Sly says, tenuously.

"At Stamports University."

"Wait, what?"

"Yup. Full ride too."

"Then how did you end up here?" Sly whispers.

"I was decent at soccer, and KU recruited me for their Division 2 team. But I didn't want to go here because of that. I chose to come here because it's only two hours away from my hometown."

"You wanted to be close to your family?"

"I wanted to be close to *her*, Juliet. So I gave up that scholarship."

"Oh," Sly says, cuddling closer. I think he knows what's coming next.

"We spent weeks learning about each other's lives. I discovered she was separated from her husband because he didn't make her happy. She let it slip one night when we were going over my essays at her house. Yes, I went to her house a few times. One night, one thing led to another...and we kissed. Nothing more, just some passionate kissing. It wasn't my first kiss, but I was hoping she would be my last, because I fell hard. I was a naive teenager, what can ya do?" I chuckle humorlessly.

"Then what happened?"

"The next week, I skipped prom, telling my

friends I was sick. I didn't have a date anyway. I went to Juliet's house. I was going to tell her I wanted to be with her. But she wouldn't let me in. Her...husband was back."

"No," Sly says gravely.

"Yup. She essentially told me to fuck off, I was her student, it was wrong, and whatever connection we had was a mistake." I laugh out loud at my own expense. "I thought because we had so much in common that it was true love. But in hindsight, it was a stupid schoolboy crush, I know."

"I wasn't going to say that," Sly says. I turn my head and expect to see his look of pity. Instead there's...a caring look. "Omar, I'm sorry you went through that."

"Yeah, well..." I clear my throat and put my hand back in his. "When I went to KU, I made friends with some frat guys immediately. There was plenty of booze and girls to go around at their parties, so I kind of lost myself in that the first month. I just didn't wanna see her face. I didn't want to remember how she tasted, how she made me feel understood. That was kind of where my reputation started."

"You didn't want to feel anything," Sly whispers.

I nod, because of course he doesn't judge me. Sly O'Rourke is really the best person I know.

"Juliet had feelings for me, for sure. But looking back, I can see she was just lonely, stuck in a rocky marriage. I was this new, young, hot thing giving her all this attention." I chuckle again at my own pathetic self. "I was an idiot to think she would leave her husband for me."

"You're not an idiot." Sly is gazing at me with this heart-wrenching sincerity. "I'm sorry she hurt you, Omar. You deserve to find the real deal, that perfect someone who values all of you for the amazing person you are."

"Thank you." I lean forward and capture Sly's lips with mine. I feel the hope of his words as he kisses me slowly. I hope Sly is that perfect person destined for me, but I don't dare say that out loud. We spend the rest of the night cuddling, kissing, and, as promised, not having sex. We don't say much more before we both drift off to sleep. When I'm holding Sly in my arms, there isn't much to say.

26: Sly

I wake up curled against a warm body and almost freak out before I remember who it is. Omar looks so peaceful, and the early dawn light makes his features look even more beautiful. Fuck, how could I ever stay away from this gorgeous, sweet, athletic man?

I gaze at his perfect chest and pristine abs with smatterings of hair rising and falling slowly. I notice the massive tent in his blue boxers, even as he's sleeping, and it gets me hard as well. I'm salivating at the sight of Omar lying here, and I long to do more with him. While I'm not yet ready for sex, I can have a little fun, right?

As if he's read my mind, Omar's eyes flutter open. "Mm...hey, sexy." He smiles in that half-asleep state of mind that only occurs before seven a.m.

"Hey, yourself." I try to sound hot despite my croaking morning voice.

"I should probably get going," Omar says, looking up at the ceiling. "Don't wanna be here when the rest of my team shows up. I'll probably get the overprotective older brother routine from both Steven *and* Ravi."

I chuckle. "Yeah, we can break the news later." I look back down at his hard bulge. "But first...I was thinking..." I walk two fingers down his perfect abs getting tantalizingly close to his shorts.

"What?" He smiles, and his hips are already jutting upward.

"While I deprived you of sex last night, I could... ya know..." I grin and touch his hardness over his underwear. "Help you out before you go?"

"Mmm..." He closes his eyes. No arguments here! "Are you sure, babe?"

I love hearing him call me that. "If you're down." I take the liberty of pulling his cock out of his fly; it's beautiful, just like I remember.

"Uhh..." He rolls his hips and I wanna hear him moan every day for the rest of my life. I used to watch porn, trying to feel something, but to no avail. But this? This is a sound from the most amazing person I've ever met, and it thrills me to no end.

Just because I'm gray-ace doesn't mean I don't want to please my man!

"Do you want me to get you off too?" Omar asks. His eyes are shut, and his hips continue to thrust into my hand. So considerate!

"No," I whisper. I stroke and tease and grip his hardness in all the places I know I like. "This is for you, babe."

"Mmmokay..." he says with a massive smile.

"You are...so sexy." I keep jerking him slowly, and I feel him get harder. It won't be much longer now.

"Uhh...fuck, Sylvester."

"Come for me, Omar," I whisper.

His eyes flutter open, all white, with his pupils rolled back. He's lost in the ecstasy I'm giving him. He moves his hips along to the rhythm of my strokes. His chest rises rapidly, and his abs clench.

"Fuck!" he grunts, gripping my pillow behind him. His cock pulses and he thrusts up one last time before he shoots. I continue to jerk him as he moans, launching volleys of semen between his perfect pecs, abs, then my hand.

Once his breathing is back to normal, his eyes open. "That...was incredible."

I smirk. "Glad my handiwork was appreciated, Alligator."

He reaches up and kisses me. His right hand plays with my own erection through my pajamas, but I squirm away. "Ah..."

"Oh, sorry, I forgot," Omar says. "Wasn't sure if you...wanted me to."

"I'm...not really...I mean you're sexy! And...and I enjoyed it! But I'm not in the mood for..."

"It's okay babe!" he says, because of course he doesn't mind. He puts his hand on my cheek and pulls me in for a quick kiss. "I'll never, for the rest of my life, force you into any sexual activity you don't want."

My heart lights up at hearing his words. They sound suspiciously like a long-term commitment, but we have plenty of hurdles to jump through first. "I promise to respect your wishes too," I reply.

"Good. Though I doubt I'll ever say no to a morning hand job!" We both giggle as he shucks off his messy boxers and gets up. "Guess I'm going home commando!" He laughs as he wipes the mess off his body with his underwear and balls it up.

He puts on his pants and I open the door only for us both to see Ravi hunched over the coffee table. He's sifting through a grocery bag and doesn't see us—thank God—but this means Steven isn't far behind him. "Uh, Sly, is that you?" Ravi asks loudly, and I immediately shut the door.

"What the hell?" I whisper while Omar frantically puts on his shirt. "They weren't supposed to be home until later!"

"Shit!" He looks around my small room. "Can I jump out the window?"

"We're way high up. I don't want you to bust your sexy ass!"

"You think it's sexy?" He smirks and looks down at his butt.

"Focus!"

"Right." I open the door a crack and peer through to see Ravi and my brother putting away groceries. Just then, Landon walks by and stares at me in horror. Behind me, Omar's face is also crowding the doorway, so I can only assume Landon's spotted him.

I shut the door on us. "Shit, I think Landon saw us," I whisper, panicking.

"It's okay. He's on our side. He knows that we hooked up."

"He does? Who else knows? The president? TMZ? Dateline?"

"You're still so cute when you're panicking." He kisses me on the cheek, and it doesn't do anything to stop my freak-out, but it's still nice.

We both peer through the door again to see Landon still staring at us. He looks back at Ravi and Steven, then back at us. "Uhh...guys," Landon announces. "I have something to show you!"

Shit. I shut the door and try to take deep breaths. Before I can get mad at Landon for outing us, I hear his voice practically yelling into my door. "Ravi, Steven...can you both come into my room? My. Room. And I'll show you...that *thing.*"

I raise my eyebrows. "I think he's creating a diversion for us!" Omar whispers, and I smile. After a beat, I open the door. The coast is clear.

"Go!" I smack Omar's firm ass to get him to dash through the living room. Once he quietly closes the front door, I take a calming breath. What a way to start the morning—my first ever hand job and sneaking a guy my brother wouldn't approve of out the door. I truly am getting the full college experience here at KU.

A few seconds later, Ravi and Steven walk out of Landon's room, which is right next to mine.

"Those were very nice pictures of '*The Christmas Picturesque*' show," Ravi says.

"But why did we have to be in *your* room to see them?" Steven asks, looking annoyed.

"Because...I want all your attention...because of my massive ego." Landon gives me a pointed look. "Hey, Sly."

"Save your ego for Dane," Steven says. Then he turns to me. "Hey. We forgot the almond milk."

"Sorry," Ravi says.

"I'll forgive you eventually," I reply, laughing uncomfortably. Landon looks at me smugly while the three of them go to the kitchen to move more groceries around. I take another relieved breath and walk into my room.

I sit there for not even two minutes before

Landon peeks his cocky blond head through the door frame. "Hey, roomie."

"Ugh," I whine, knowing what's coming.

He closes the door and walks in. "How was your winter break?"

I stand up and pace around. "It was...good." I subtly kick Omar's dirty boxers underneath the bed, hoping Landon doesn't notice.

"Anything...exciting happen?"

I frown. "Nothing of note."

"Hey, I spent a lot of winter break with my boyfriend." He leans on my desk and crosses his arms. "Which, I guess, is something we have in common now?"

I lower my jaw and push up my glasses in annoyance. "What do you want, Landon?"

"Look, I just wanna be genuine when I say this: Omar is one of my best friends, and I love and support him like a brother. But so is Ravi. And we both know he's just an extension of Steven."

I shrug and look out the window, feeling anxious. "Okay..."

"I'm just saying your secret's safe with me." He moves in to touch my arm, but I pull back, and he drops his hand. "But I don't want to have to cover for you two forever. I can't keep lying to Ravi."

"Alright, alright." I look down. Landon actually does have a point. "We'll...tell them very soon."

"Good man." He goes and places his hand on my doorknob, but pauses and turns back to me. "You know, I can tell he really likes you. So...I hope you two stay together."

I smile, and I know my face just got redder. It seems on some level I always wanted the approval of one of

Omar's best friends.

"Do you guys need any condoms or lube?" His smug grin is back as he opens the door.

"Get the fuck out of my room," I whisper, biting back a smile.

27: Omar

We wait three whole days before we decide to make things official. Sly and I text and chat constantly, and we decide on a formal announcement at his apartment. I invite Kareem, too, all under the guise of a small pizza party. We each mention there will be beer and board games to play, just for us soccer boys.

Now is the moment of truth because everyone is in the apartment living room. Ravi and Steven are on the couch next to Kareem, each with a beer in hand. Landon is in the large chair with Dane in his lap—he practically lives here since he and Landon are all honeymoon-phase-inseparable. *Fuck, I want that with Sly.*

"It's going to be fine." Hearing my boyfriend whisper snaps me back to reality. We're both standing at the doorway, out of earshot. I want him to hold me and tell me it will all work out. Landon is on our side, but if Steven disapproves, I know it will hurt both Sly and me.

"I know," I reply. "I'm not nervous. Why would you think I'm nervous?"

"You're tapping your toes and biting your

thumbnail."

"Oh." I immediately drop my hand and shove them both in my pockets. My feet are still going, though.

"Look, nothing's going to change, except now we get to be out in the open," Sly whispers. His beautiful brown eyes behind his glasses have a calming effect on me. "We got this, Alligator." He grins, and I feel a wave of affection and relief.

We walk in front of the TV and get everyone's attention. "Hey, guys! So...you're probably wondering why we called you here," I announce, standing next to Sly.

"We live here," Ravi replies.

"And I thought it was just *your* announcement, Omar?" Kareem asks.

"Yeah, why *is* Sly standing next to you?" Steven asks, a hint of suspicion in his voice.

Sly and I nod at each other, and then he takes my hand. "We would like to announce to you all that...Omar and I are...in a relationship."

The five dudes in front of us just stare back in silence. You can probably hear the sound of my heartbeat. It's that quiet. I awkwardly shift from foot to foot.

"Wait, what?" Ravi asks, finally breaking the silence.

"Sly and I are...together." I turn to my man. "Romantically. I was told it's what you do when you like someone." He grins at me, and his cheeks get redder. Sly O'Rourke is so precious to me I don't care what these guys will throw at us; I want the world to know he's mine.

"Huh? Since when? Wait...w-what?" Steven asks, sputtering. His eyes keep darting between the two of us like we're doing an elaborate but horrifying magic trick.

"He's my boyfriend, Steven," Sly says. "We wanted you all to know first." Steven is still staring at us open-mouthed.

"Aww, that's great!" Dane says. "I don't really know you guys that well, but...I'm happy for you two!" He turns to Landon in the chair. "We're happy for them, right?" His voice is lower and he sounds like he really needs Landon to take the lead on this.

"Yes," Landon replies. "We're both really happy for you. And uh..." He turns to his left. "We *all* are, right, Ravi?"

"Uh..." Ravi looks to Steven, who still looks like a fish mounted on a wall. "Steven? Babe?"

"I just don't..." Steven looks down, eyebrows furrowed. "I mean, I had my suspicions but..." His eyes meet mine. "Why *my* little brother? Out of *all* the people at school you could date, why *him?*"

"I'm standing right here," Sly says. He's looking up at the ceiling but he sounds pissed. I grip his hand tighter.

"Steven, I *like* Sly. He gets me." We smile at each other and I rub his arm up and down. "We got closer when I directed the play, and when the year ended, we realized...we were the highlight of each other's semester."

"Aww, that is *way* cute," Dane remarks, cuddling closer to Landon.

"Not even winning the regional championship?" Ravi asks incredulously.

"If someone made you pick between Steven and the championship, which would you pick?" I point at him accusatorily.

"Steven, duh," he says without hesitating, putting his hand on Steven's knee.

"Well, okay then!" I'm sure I sound irritated now.

Steven gets up and takes a deep breath. "Sly, can I talk to you in private?"

"No," he says firmly. He laces his fingers in mine and grips me tighter. "Anything you can say to me, you can say in front of my boyfriend." He points to Kareem, then Landon. "And he tells me you guys are his bros, his ride-or-die's. If you mean that much to Omar, then I accept you all, too. It's why I wanted us *all* here to talk."

"Wow, that's like the most I've ever heard you say," Ravi mutters, sipping his beer.

"I knew there was no such thing as free pizza," Dane says, and Landon chuckles.

"Alright..." Steven buzzes his lips and puts his hands in front of them like he's praying. He pauses for a moment, then looks back at Sly. "Sly, you're my little brother —"

"Don't *'little brother'* me, Steven," Sly interrupts. I hold him closer; the last thing I want is a sibling altercation.

"Then let me finish, Sylvester!" he barks. He takes a deep breath with his eyes closed. "Look, I just want you to make sure you know what you're doing."

"We're doing just fine, thanks," Sly says, gritting his teeth.

"Does Omar...treat you right?"

"I'm also standing right here," I mutter.

"Yes!" Sly exclaims.

"Does he treat you like you're royalty? Like you're the best person in his life?"

"Yes! He's the only one I've ever wanted and the only person who's ever made me so deliriously happy all the time!" Sly is nearly shouting. "Please just be cool with this and let me live my life!"

"I *am* cool with it! I just wanted to know my little brother is being taken care of because you deserve the best! If that really is Omar, then I'm *HAPPY* for you!"

"Okay, then *THANK YOU!*" They're both shouting now, taking deep breaths, and the rest of us are just watching.

There's a long heavy silence until finally, Steven and Sly, both nearly mirror images of each other, burst out laughing. They dive into each other's arms, hugging, and we all join in their laughter.

Steven ruffles Sly's hair, and Sly pats it back down. "I guess our family events just got a lot bigger, little brother."

"It's these soccer boys, Stevie. *Our* soccer boys," Sly says, smiling. He steps back and I pull him into a side hug. "We never stood a chance staying away from them."

"No, I suppose we didn't. And now we're stuck with them." Steven flashes a brilliant smile at Ravi who puts his arm around him. They make heart eyes at each other, and I know everything is gonna be fine.

"That is too cute," Dane coos. Landon nods and hugs Dane tighter. I notice Kareem is the only one quietly drinking beer as the laughter dies down.

"Great! So we're all good!" I announce. "Kareem...you're good too, right?"

We all turn to him, and he slowly puts his beer down.

"No. No, I'm not." He gets up and briskly walks out of their apartment, shutting the door and leaving the rest of us silent in his wake.

28: Sly

I didn't see that coming. Kareem? The quiet, straight one? *He's* the one pissed that Omar and I are dating? Never a dull moment in this apartment, I swear.

After thirty uncomfortable seconds of silence, Omar clears his throat. "I should go see if he's out there."

"No," I say. "Let me."

"Are you sure?" Omar asks.

"He'll be expecting you. I've never actually talked to him, and I think I can manage." Omar looks at me skeptically. "Future social worker, remember?"

"You *do* give really good advice," Landon adds. "You saw issues I didn't even know I had."

"Like what?" Dane asks. Landon cringes.

"I got this," I whisper to Omar. I lean my head to touch his forehead.

"Okay," he concedes. "But if you're not back in ten minutes, I'm going out there to kick his ass." I give him a quick peck on the cheek.

"Gross," Steven says with a smile. I chuckle and

leave the living room.

Closing the apartment door behind me, I see Kareem sitting at the top of the cement stairs. It's a cold January night, and one building light shines above us.

"Man, can we not—" Kareem stops himself when he notices me sitting down. "Oh...I thought you were one of the guys."

"Hey, I *am* a guy," I chide with a grin.

"You know what I mean," he replies, smiling. He turns back to face the darkened street, and I do the same. There aren't even cars any driving by, just the sound of crickets to keep us company. After a moment of tense quiet, he finally pipes up again. "You should know...it's not a gay thing."

"I know."

"Really?" He side-eyes me with a look of skepticism.

"Yeah. Ravi told me you've been nothing but supportive of him and my brother."

"Well, duh. They're my boys. I want us all to be happy."

"So do you want to tell me what that was all about? Because Omar could really use your support right now."

"I know," Kareem mutters. He pulls his phone out of his pocket. "I want to show you something."

A moment later, he scrolls through his photos and puts an image in front of me: it's a younger group of guys in a grainy photo on a soccer field. The fit black guy with a smile on his face in the middle looks like Kareem, but definitely isn't.

171

"What is this?"

"That's my brother and his best friends. He was on the soccer team at KU too, nine years ago."

"Oh, that's awesome...Right?"

Kareem puts away his phone and shrugs. "My brother used to tell me they were the best of friends. I'm nine years younger than him, so of course I looked up to him. I would watch the soccer games, and I'd see him and his boys when they hung out at our house. That sense of brotherhood...I wanted that so badly."

"Okay," I reply. I think I know where he's going, but he's on a roll, so I'm not stopping him.

"And I actually got it!" Kareem laughs, staring at his shoes. "I became co-captain. I found Ravi, Landon, Omar, and all the other guys on our team. We became a soccer band of brothers. Being with these guys is a dream come true."

"That sounds awesome. Omar sees you guys as family too," I say.

"Yeah, well...I asked my brother about his friends last summer, the guys in the picture. It turns out he doesn't even talk to them anymore. They grew apart after graduation." Kareem puts his hand over his eyes like he doesn't want to see me. "We're in our last semester. I loved being regional champions, and I love Stacia. Ravi would do anything for your brother, and Landon is back with his boy, too."

"And now I'm with Omar," I say, reading his mind. "The guy who swore he would never settle down."

Kareem looks at me. "Look, it's not personal. I'm sure you're great. Omar seems super happy with you. It's just...everything's changing so fast. These guys are my brothers, but now we're all in serious relationships, even

Omar. Once we graduate, are we going to grow apart too?"

I bite my lip trying to choose my next words carefully. "I can't predict what's to come. No one can. Your brother and his friends growing apart is definitely not a vision of your future, not unless you let it be."

He looks down but doesn't respond, so I continue, "You have one final semester together as a team. You can enjoy it and make memories for a lifetime, or you can squander it and *definitely* grow apart. Again, I don't know where you and those guys will be in a year or two. I don't even know where my relationship is heading." I clear my throat and try not to let that realization shake me. This is about Kareem.

"But what I do know is your best friend Omar is in there right now, and he wants to know you accept his relationship. Because those guys all think the world of you, too."

Kareem finally looks me in the eye and smiles. "You're a good guy." He holds out his fist and I bump it, which Omar told me is the universal sign of athletics forgiveness. "Steven is right when he says you're smart and capable of anything."

I feel my face get redder. "What?"

"Your brother. According to Ravi, all he does is talk about how much he admires all the decisions you make. And how you're going to make an awesome social worker because you make human connections all the time." Kareem gets up and shrugs, and I stand as well trying to hide my smile.

"I didn't know…Steven thought that about me. I was just in there begging him to accept my decision to date Omar."

Kareem smiles. "Take it from someone who also has an older brother; I can tell he respects the crap out of you." His words make my heart fill with satisfaction. Steven's never said that to me, and I didn't know I needed to hear it. In a dramatic night of revealing truths, this one takes the cake.

"Thanks. And whatever happens, I'm sure you and the guys will remain friends years from now."

"I thought you weren't psychic," he jokes. We're both chuckling when the front door opens and Omar appears.

"Everything okay out here?"

"Has it been ten minutes already?" I ask.

"Nine, but I wanted to make sure Kareem didn't push you down the stairs."

"Fuck outta here, I would never," Kareem says. He puts his hands in his pockets and looks down. "I'm sorry if I said I wasn't supportive. I am. Sly is a cool guy, and we should go on a double date some time."

Omar's eyebrows jump. "Thanks, man, no worries." They grin at each other and do the bro side-hug and we all trail back inside. We finally get around to playing some drinking card games and ordering that pizza.

For the next few hours, we have a good time, laughing and telling jokes all around. I sit on the floor with Omar and he holds my hand for most of the night. I don't have to worry about Steven catching us or anyone judging us. I get to simply live in the moment with the guy I'm crazy about. It's the most comfortable I've ever been.

I don't know where my relationship will be in seven months when Omar's long gone, and that scares the shit out of me. But that's a problem for tomorrow. Tonight, like

Kareem, I just need to be in the now with the dudes around me that have become my family.

I've got a great boyfriend, new friends, and my brother accepts me. It's everything I came to KU for and so much more.

29: Omar

I've discovered the secret to time travel; in order to accelerate two-and-a-half months in five seconds, just be in your final semester of college and dating an amazing guy. I have no idea how it's almost May; all I know is I want it all to slow down. The spring semester of soccer isn't as important as the fall season, especially since we're coming off being regional champions. I'm finishing up all my degree requirements, and I even had time to be Aggie's assistant director again for the spring musical. I want to pursue theater arts after I graduate, so I've applied for graduate programs in New York City.

I couldn't have done any of this without the support of my fantastic boyfriend. Things have been going well for us. We watch movies with his brother and Ravi at their place. Sometimes we go on double dates with Kareem or Landon and their partners. We haven't done anal, and Sly barely wants me to get him off, but I don't mind—he gets me off plenty, and I am certainly satisfied!

The nights I hold him as I sleep are the best, and I feel myself falling for him. I can see a real future with him: the ring, the wedding bells, the white picket fence, and all of the romance clichés. I'm not sure if he feels the same. All of this is so new for both of us. Still, with every kiss and every night spent together, the kindling of hope that he loves me back burns brighter.

I walk out of the final performance for *The Wizard of Oz* feeling energized. Taking a bow with the cast and having Aggie give me a shout-out on stage as her assistant director was a thrilling experience, and I'll never forget it. Some audience members congratulate me in the hallway, and I nod politely as I try to subtly look for the one person who's always on my mind. I finally spot him at the end of the hallway holding a manila envelope and beaming at me.

I run up to Sly and dramatically hug and spin him around. We both giggle, not caring who's around. "You were amazing, Alligator!"

"Aw shucks, I wasn't singing with the cast," I reply.

"No, but I could see all the little touches of this show that were yours."

"Of course Sly O'Rourke is more impressed by the technical aspects of the production than by the actors." We both chuckle.

"Maybe because I have the hots for the assistant director," he purrs. I lean in to kiss him but I stop when I see some folks in my periphery.

I immediately bolt away, and Sly turns to his right to meet my dad, in a suit, looking at us, sternly. Smiling next to him are my mom and nineteen-year-old sister.

"Omar sweetie, great job!" My mom pulls me into a hug while my sister taps my shoulder.

"That was fun. I really enjoyed it," my sister says.

"Thanks, Mom, thanks, Roma. Dad?"

"It was good," he says. He clears his throat, then points behind me. "Your uh...*friend* in the glasses ran away."

I turn back to see Sly intently fiddling on his phone a few yards away, leaning against a wall. I don't miss my dad's emphasis on the word 'friend.' While I told my parents I don't have a preference for girls or guys years ago, I'm not sure if they remember.

Turning back around, I smile at my parents. "Yeah well, he brought me something I need to show you all. Can we go to dinner?"

"Only if you're buying," my sister says, grinning.

"I'll be using Mom's credit card," I say with a shrug, and they all smile.

"We'll see you at that diner we like," Mom says. Dad just nods and looks perceptively at Sly in the distance, then they all leave.

I make my way back to my man. "Shit, what did your parents say?"

"Relax, babe," I reply. I take the envelope. "I'm going to dinner with them now, just as we planned."

"I've never met a girl's parents before. Err, a guy's parents..." He blushes and pushes up his glasses in the way that drives me crazy. "Do I look presentable?"

"You"—I kiss him, hard—"look amazing. But I gotta get going. Wish me luck?" I wag the envelope for emphasis.

"You don't need it, Omar. You're talented, hard-working, and the best guy I know."

My heart flutters hearing him say those words. I want to tell him I love him, but instead, I kiss his cheek, then walk away. I've got one massive hurdle I still need to overcome.

"What is all this?" Dad asks. We've just finished eating dessert at the diner. I pass around papers to each of the three of them.

"It's my post-college life plan itinerary," I announce. "Dad, I know how much you love typed-up plans, timetables, and cost-benefit ratios."

"I'm not...always into them," Dad says.

"Yes, you are," Mom says, staring at him skeptically.

"You really are, Dad," Roma adds. I know I win this round of logic.

I smile. "As you can see, I've outlined my next three years. I've...been accepted into New York Manhattan University's theater arts program."

"Theater arts?" Mom says, looking over my itinerary.

"For real?" my sister asks.

"Yes," I reply. The nerves are starting to kick in. "I want to...produce and direct live stage productions."

"And how will you pay for all this?" Dad asks.

"As you can see in paragraph 3a..." I grin as they all look down at their papers. "Professor Hark helped me with a small scholarship for the program. There are local jobs all over New York, and our cousin Firass said I could take over his apartment's lease when he graduates."

"The gay cousin?" Dad asks, still looking down.

I roll my eyes. "Yes, Dad."

"Are you sure there's a future in this?" Mom asks, her tone

laced with sincerity.

"Yes, Mom. My English degree will actually be put to good use."

"Well, that certainly is true," she says. My parents are still staring at my itinerary.

"I think it's a great idea," Roma adds. "You did a baller job directing that play."

"Thanks, sister."

"Look, we all thought it was baller," Dad says. Roma and I bite back a laugh at him using slang. "But is this really a viable career option?"

I clear my throat and sit up straight. "Under table 2a, you can see a list of individuals with careers in theater, many of whom are KU alumni."

"Wow," my mom says as they all look at the table. I know I've nearly convinced my mom and sister, and now I just need my dad on board.

After a few minutes, he finally looks at me. "You did this outline yourself?"

I shrug. "Yes, well...I had some help."

"Was it from that cute guy in glasses?" Roma teases.

"Hey, that cute guy is my...friend." I feel my face get warmer.

"This isn't about your boyfriend or girlfriend, Omar," Mom says. "We just need to make sure you can take care of yourself."

"I can!" I turn to Dad. "Any questions, send them my way, but Dad, this is it. You once asked me for my life plan, and I think I can make this happen."

He stares me down, and my mom and sister look at him. All we hear are the clanging of plates at the tables around us. After thirty long seconds, Dad finally speaks. "You'll need to make connections and brush up on your résumé."

I smile, and my heart speeds up. "Absolutely."

"Make sure theaters all over New York, not just in Manhattan, know about your skills."

"My skills, yes." I nod rapidly. Is he saying what I think he's saying?

"It's going to take long hours of working to pay for school and theater internships wherever you can get them."

"Yes, of course!" My foot is tapping rapidly as it dawns on me—this is my dad's actual approval!

"We can't keep paying for all your books and classes," Dad says.

"I swear, I'll restock books at the library or help coach soccer. Whatever job accepts me."

"And you need to check in with us regularly," Mom says.

"And one day you'll get us free tickets to Broadway musicals," Roma adds, grinning.

"If I pull this off, you can star in a production for all I care." We both laugh.

"You *will* pull this off," Dad says, seriously. "Because you're an Odom. We worked hard moving to this country to make sure you kids succeed."

I'm almost in tears. "Thanks, Dad. I'm gonna make you proud."

"We love you, son. You're gonna do great." Mom starts to sniff, and I hope she avoids the waterworks.

"Mom and Dad totally cried when you bowed on stage," Roma mutters, smiling.

"We did not!" Dad says. Our table bursts out laughing, and I feel so blessed to have such an open-minded and supportive family.

30: Sly

When Omar comes over that night, I quickly drag him into my room without saying a word. I lock the door behind him and huff while he stares at me perplexed. "I've been dying to know what happened," I whisper. "What did your parents say about the plan you made?"

"You mean the plan *we* made? I couldn't have organized that life path without your help." He smiles and leans in.

"Okay, okay, so what did they say?" I whine as he moves closer to my mouth. He kisses me gently, and just like every other time, there's fireworks.

Pulling back, he whispers, "They loved the plan and are ready to support me in any way."

"No way."

"Yes!" He giggles, his breath on my face and I break out in a smile.

"Omar, that's amazing!" I fling myself at him and grip him hard. A year ago, I could never imagine myself choosing to hug anyone, least of all one of Steven's soccer friends.

"And it's all because of you," he says, pulling back. "You showed me what true passion is, that I could pursue it long term. I can never thank you enough."

I beam at him and hug him again. "Your love is thanks enough, Alligator." I feel his shoulders stiffen in my arms. *Shit. Why did I say that?*

He lets go again and stares at me in horror. "How...did you know?"

"What?" I ask, my face feeling flaming hot.

"Is it obvious that I love you? Because I do, I was just trying to play it cool." He looks down and chuckles self-consciously. "You don't have to say it back. I didn't wanna put pressure on you."

I laugh and put my hands on his face. "And you never do. And that's how I know you love me." He finally lifts his head. "Which is good because I love you, too."

The smile that grows on his face will forever be seared in my brain. "Really?"

I nod. "You're talented, and incredible, Omar. I've been falling in love with you for a while now. And I'm so proud of you for telling your family about your life plan."

"Well, that's really convenient because I love you, too."

We kiss some more, and my pulse starts to race, and not just because Omar is sexy. I pull back and search his face. "Omar, it okay if..."

"What is it?"

I close my eyes. "Tonight I...think I want to have sex. I want you to top me."

He doesn't answer, so I open my eyes to see him staring at me, expressionless.

"Are you sure?"

"Babe, we've been dating for months. You've made me feel more comfortable than anyone." I peck his lips. "I want my first time to be with you." *And all my other times, too.*

"I know you're gray-ace...and I know you don't always want it."

"Well..." I feel a blush on my face. "I kinda... *prepared* myself. Down there. Knowing whatever happened tonight with your family, you might need either a pick-me-up or a celebration."

He chuckles and kisses me again. "You're ready for me, huh?"

"Omar," I whisper, leaning into kiss his neck. He tilts his head back and moans. "You turn me on so much. I know I'm not always into it, but...I am right now."

This seems to awaken the animal inside him. The next two minutes are a blur of taking off our clothes while trying to keep our lips on each other. Once he gets the supplies, I pull him in and, chest to chest, kiss him hard, my tongue meeting his. I stroke both of us, our cocks dancing next to each other, until we're ready. Finally, I lie back on the edge of the bed, and Omar squirts some lube in his hand.

"Tell me everything you need, babe." He rolls the condom on. "Fast, slow, or we can stop. I just want you to be good."

"You always take care of me," I reply softly. *How did I luck out winning over this thoughtful and sexy man?* "Kiss me, babe." He leans over my body and obliges. His mouth tastes sweet, and I can't get over how natural it all feels. I used to hate the idea of being held down, but now I don't want Omar to be apart from me, ever. I don't know what will happen in two months when he's living in New York City. I just know I need him now.

He fingers me for a bit. It's weird, but he's using a generous helping of lube, so he glides in easily. It certainly helps that I cleaned myself out an hour ago. Then, when I say I'm ready, he eases in. It's strange at first, burns a little, but…

Oh.

Oh fuck. Omar Odom, the gorgeous soccer star, is inside me.

Losing my virginity isn't quite as comfortable as I'd like, but Omar looks so sexy as he begins to thrust. Pretty soon, he hits that sweet spot, and my hardness seems to double in strength.

"Fuck," I moan, shutting my eyes.

"Should I stop?"

"Hell no!" I reply, and we both chuckle. He continues to fuck me in the most delicious way. His sweat drips onto me, and I don't even care—it's Omar, *my* Omar, we could never be too close.

He fucks me for a few minutes more. Sometimes it's hot, sometimes there's discomfort, but it's always evident that he's enjoying the ride. "You feel so good, babe…" Omar moans.

I don't feel close, so I chase an instinct. "Omar." He stops, mid-thrust, at the sound of his name.

"I want you to shoot all over me."

He grins and slowly eases out of me. After ripping the condom off, he lies on top of me, covering my body again. I jerk us both off, kissing the salty skin of his neck as he grips the sheets and grinds into me.

"This feels so good, Sly…"

"Fuck yeah…I want you all over me, babe.

Fucking let it out…all over me."

This sets him off. He groans and juts into me one last time before I feel his cock pulse. Seeing him come all over me lights me up and I'm orgasming seconds later. We've intertwined into one mass of moans and stuttering hips—it's the hottest thing I've ever been a part of.

He rolls next to me and I lean over to kiss him slowly. For me, sex isn't always good, but being with Omar has never felt anything but right. I continue to put my lips on his while he slowly drifts off to sleep. I didn't think sex would ever be in the cards for me. As usual, Omar is the perfect exception to all of my rules.

"And we have one final team dinner before graduation," Omar says. He scoops up the last of his frozen yogurt.

"Sweet," I reply. It's the day after I lost my virginity—*Woohoo!*—and Omar and I are at the Student Union. We found a corner table and are happily eating desserts together.

"Alright, I'm gonna go, babe." He stands up, but I don't join him. "Can I walk you to the library?"

"No thanks, I'm meeting Charles here real soon." His face scrunches up, but I just chuckle. "We have to talk about the apartment we're sharing next year."

"You're sure he's not going to try to make a pass at you?"

I roll my eyes but grin. "He's straight. And just a friend. More importantly, I love you."

He smiles and leans in to kiss me slowly. "That's what I like to hear, babe. Catch you later."

After Omar leaves, the loneliness in my heart starts to set in. He says he loves me now, but will it be enough when he's in New York? I'm sure he can find tons of guys or girls who actually like sex in the big city. I definitely won't be able to find someone better, but someone as beautiful and amazing as him could replace me any day of the week.

My lamenting is cut short when Charles finally arrives with a plate of pizza. We talk logistics for a bit, and it does the trick of getting my mind off Omar. He talks about what video games he's bringing and how he doesn't smoke anything, so it sounds like we'll fit well as roommates.

"And assuming she still wants me around, Celia will be over in my room on occasion," Charles says, finishing his food.

"Oh yeah, sure," I reply. I stare at my now empty cup of yogurt.

"And it's cool if Omar comes over, too."

"Okay," I say, looking around. This conversation isn't helping anymore.

"How are you guys doing?" I look at Charles and he seems sincere.

"We're..." I shrug, unsure of what to say. "He's graduating, so we'll see how well our relationship goes over the summer."

"Dude, that guy is *crazy* about you. I'll be surprised if he doesn't find a way to visit you weekly." Charles laughs and gets up to throw away his trash. "You two will be fine. Alright, catch you later!"

"Later." I plaster on a fake smile.

That's yet another problem. Omar needs to focus on hustling for his career. He can't do that if he keeps visiting me here at KU. I know he loves me, but I think we'll need to take an extended break if we both want to be successful. I doubt Omar will agree, so I won't say anything for now. I'm going to let him be happy and enjoy his graduation season because all those boys deserve it.

31: Omar

"Our next speech is from one of the captains of the men's soccer team. Please join me in welcoming Ravi Metta!" The dean moves to the side as Ravi walks on stage in cap and gown. I adjust my own square hat then join the rest of the crowd in applause. Landon is hollering next to me, and Kareem is on my other side, clapping and grinning. The Athletics Center is packed with thousands of people, all graduates and their loved ones. I don't see Sly in the audience, but I know he wouldn't miss this for the world; after all, Steven is in another section graduating as well.

"Fellow students, families, faculty, and loved ones," Ravi announces into the microphone at the podium. He looks up at the audience and flashes that million-dollar smile. "We did it."

The crowd goes wild like he scored a game-winning goal. After a whole minute, the cheering dies down and he gets to continue his speech. "As a kid, I was taught that magic isn't real. It's just make-believe. But after these past four years, I disagree. Magic is alive and well, and it definitely exists here at Korham University. This school *has* magic, and all it takes is a few years to put in the work and studying...and tuition, courtesy of our parents."

There's a roar of laughter, and I chuckle. "This place has to be magic. How else can you describe a school where the shy, introverted, dark-skinned boy who loved soccer could transform into the best version of himself? What other place has dance majors mingle with jocks until they fall in love? It has to be magic when athletes can co-direct multiple musicals." My eyes start to sting, and I smile at Landon, who's subtly trying to wipe away a tear.

Ravi clears his throat and continues, "Before I came here, the lines were drawn in the sand of society. They put me, and so many like me, in a box. I was taught I couldn't love who I wanted to love, that I was meant only to play sports and keep my mouth shut. I stayed in my comfort zone and never made any moves to grow. But the magic of KU wouldn't allow me to stay there. I discovered the truest version of myself, and it's all thanks to KU forcing me to broaden my horizons. The culture of acceptance and diversity at this school isn't just on paper; it's alive and well. Whether you're a shy musician or spend all your time at the gym, I'd bet that KU helped find a place for you."

"My only request as you all go forward with me into adulthood is this: if you find the place that makes you happy, filled with people who will support you 100 percent...then please don't let it go. Cherish those people, hold on to them, and fight for them. Because you're fighting to love yourself, the only battle worth fighting."

The words cut me deep. Sly makes me happier than anyone, and I don't want to let him go. Ravi's eyes look wet on stage, and Landon isn't even trying to hide his crying anymore. "Whether you're an artist, athlete, academic, queer, ally, none of the above, or somehow all of it—you've felt the magic of KU. The only trick I never learned here was how to go back in time to day one and do it all over again, forging all of the friendships and loves sooner rather than later." There are some cheers and laughter, and I raise my fist and holler.

"I love this school. I love my teammates, friends, and family. Thank you, KU, for the magic of allowing me to be who I really am. And congratulations to our class of graduates."

There's a thunderous applause as he steps to the side, and the dean announces the next speech. Admittedly, I can't pay attention to the valedictorian; I'm too busy crying into the arms of Landon and Kareem, muttering how much I love them, my soccer brothers, and always will.

We must take at least 900 photos outside the Athletics Center once graduation is over. There are different permutations of the team, friends, boyfriends, girlfriends, and family members. It's blazing hot under my cap and gown, but I don't mind because this is the last time we're going to be together for a while.

In one photo, I kiss Sly hard, leaning him over, not caring who sees. Once we've pulled apart, he chuckles and caresses my cheek. "You're something else, Mr. Odom."

"You keep saying that, and it never gets old." I grin at him. I swear, in a crowd of hundreds, no one else seems to exist.

"Omar!" I turn to see Coach Dacks waving me over to another soccer team group pic, this time with the underclassmen.

"Go," Sly says. "You're still a KU soccer player for the next few minutes."

"But you said you're leaving soon with Steven and your parents for the airport?"

"Yeah, but go be with your boys."

"Okay." My face falls then picks right back up again. "Wait for me?"

He pauses, pushes up his glasses, and then nods. I smile at him and run to my team.

"Catch me boys!" I leap into Ravi, Vince, and Landon's arms, lying horizontally. They all laugh and holler as multiple photographers take a slew of wacky pictures.

"You're a heavy bastard," Vince says once they put me down.

"Yeah, you've graduated for five minutes and you already let yourself go!" Paul adds, pinching my cheek.

"You think you get to be sassy now that you're co-captains?" I wag my finger at them. Everyone laughs, including Coach Dacks.

"Hey, you recommended us to Coach!" Paul says with a shrug.

"And I'd do it again," Kareem says, and Ravi nods in agreement.

Our faces get serious. "Me, too," I add.

"Me three," Landon says, his eyes getting wet.

"I'm so proud of how much you guys have grown. Seems like just yesterday we brought you to your first frat party and now —" Ravi chokes up.

"Nope! We're not doing this anymore. No more waterworks! We had enough crying at the ceremony," Landon says.

"That was just *you*, Landee," I remark, and everyone's back to laughing. I turn to Vince and Paul. "But seriously, keep our legacy up, okay?"

"Of course, we could never forget you guys. Teammates for life," Paul replies.

"KU men's soccer for life!" Vince hollers in the air, and soon we're all chanting *"Panthers! Panthers!"*

Several minutes later, once the crowd has dissipated, I walk over to Sly, who's sitting on a bench. He's hunched over and guarded, the way he used to sit when I first met him. "Sup gorgeous?" He looks up, eyes puffy like he's been crying. "Aww, babe, I know. I cried during Ravi's speech, too." I sit down and rub his back.

"It's not that," he says, sniffing. "I'm crying because of *you*."

"What?" My eyebrows are furrowed and my pulse speeds up. Did I do something wrong in the past three weeks? We sleep together every night. We've been swamped with finals and graduation stuff, so we haven't had sex, but I thought he was cool with that.

"It's just...Omar." He bursts into tears and lands in my chest. "I love you so much."

"Aww, babe." I hold him close, almost in tears. "I love you, too."

"But you've graduated...You're...gonna be gone next year..." He sobs in my arms. We both knew I was graduating and that he would be here for another year. "They say if you love something, let it go...so I think we should just take a break."

"No," I say resolutely. I gently pull him off me and look at his puffy red eyes. "We're not doing that. This isn't how our story ends. We're not breaking up."

"But you need to focus on your career!"

"I love you, okay? You're the only person I've ever loved. I'm not quitting on us."

"But what if when you live in New York City, you find someone better? Someone who actually enjoys sex as much as you do? I refuse to make you sexually frustrated from a distance. I know a gray-ace guy isn't the ideal boyfriend for you, but—"

"Hey, *no*," I say firmly, wiping his tears. "No one is more ideal than you, you got that?" I kiss him gently. "You remember what Ravi said in his speech?"

"It was like, an hour ago, so yeah," Sly says, wiping away a tear.

"He said if you find the people that make you happy, then hold onto them. For me, that's you. *You* make me the most happy." I kiss his head and hold him close, tears welling in my eyes. "I need you, babe."

"You make me the most happy too," he mutters. "But I still don't want to hold you back while you're away."

"How about we compromise? We spend as much time as possible together before school starts. Then, if being apart from me is so bad, in six months, we can...re-evaluate our relationship."

He nods, visibly calmer. "That sounds...fair. God, you are the best, you know that?" He strokes my cheek and I try not to tear up.

"No, you are. You're really the best thing I could have ever asked for, Sylvester O'Rourke."

There's a vibration, and he checks his phone. "Shit, Steven is waiting for me. We have to leave for the flight. I'm sorry, I gotta go."

"I know." We stand up and, I embrace him hard. "I love you, Sly, okay? This isn't our final chapter. Our romance novel is just starting."

"I love you, too, Omar," he mutters into my neck. Once he pulls back, he kisses me one last time, and then he walks backwards to where his parents are waiting.

"Have a great trip!"

"Thanks!"

"Say the thing!" I shout.

I see him roll his eyes behind his glasses, and he smiles. "See you later, Alligator!"

I chuckle and wipe away a stray tear. Once he's gone, I take off my graduation cap and walk back to find my parents, both ready and scared shitless to start adulthood.

32: Sly

Almost every week for the past several months, I've asked Omar the same question over the phone: "Are you sure you don't want to date someone else where you are?" His answer is always a resolute "No." I'm surprised he isn't pissed off at me yet or hasn't broken up with me out of sheer annoyance.

We did manage to spend a decent amount of time together over the summer. I visited New York City a few times, once with Steven for a big graduation party at the Landon residence. Each time was amazing; being with Omar in the biggest city I've ever seen felt just like the movies. We never discussed how hard it would be once school started. We just lived in the moment. The old Sly used to overthink everything, but with Omar wrapped around me, the voices in my head disappeared.

This, of course, didn't work when I was back at KU. Omar's been busy hustling for his new degree, so he understandably hasn't been able to visit me. For my final year, I've mostly hung out with Charles, Celia, and some other QPU people I've met. I love KU, but I didn't think I'd miss my brother and his friends *this* much.

Without Omar around, I don't even know where we stand. He said he wanted to re-evaluate our relationship, so he would come up and visit me sometime this week. He was pretty vague about the details, and I've been busy with finals.

I'm not sure what there is to re-evaluate. I love him so much and missing him hurts so bad. It's not even like I'm guaranteed to find a grad school near him in the fall. It feels like our lives are heading in different directions. I feel guilty for doubting he cares for me. Then the guilt makes me feel like the worst boyfriend ever, and then I doubt myself even more, and the vicious cycle continues.

So this semester, I've spent a lot of free time exercising. I've gotten pretty close to Logan by proxy of being tight with Wei, and he let me train with the athletes. I needed to do anything to get my mind off Omar and the fear that he'll show up after six months and call it quits. Everywhere I went reminded me of the love of my life, but at least in the Athletics Center, I could get fit while I was longing for him.

Speaking of the Center, I'm here tonight, and the annual Athletics Formal has just wrapped up. While I'm no athlete, Logan asked me to come as part of the surprise for Wei: Logan got on one knee and popped the question in front of everyone. I admit, I got teared up watching Wei, one of my favorite people in the world, get engaged. Logan asked me to take lots of pictures for him.

Now though, I'm helping Wei and Logan clean up since all of the jocks have left. Christmas lights twinkle everywhere, and it was a gorgeous dinner dance. I feel that third-wheel vibe since the two faculty lovebirds won't stop bumping hips and giggling as they remove trash.

Their love reminds me so much of Omar and how much I miss him. I guess it's written all over my face because Wei walks over to me and Logan leaves us.

"Hey Sly...you okay, buddy?"

"I'm great. I should be asking you, Mr. Got-that-ring."

We both chuckle, and he looks at his diamond engagement band. "I'm still in shock. It's lovely. Logan has more money than he knows what to do with. But stop deflecting. Tell old Professor Wong what's wrong."

We sit down at an empty table near the courtside exit, and I take a deep breath. "It's the same old story. I miss Omar. Everything reminds me of him."

"You'll see him again soon, I know it."

"He said he would visit KU this week, but he was pretty vague about it."

"That's something to look forward to."

"Yeah..." I pick off a stray piece of confetti from my slacks. "Maybe I should just go home, call it a night."

"No!" Wei yelps, standing up. "You...you can't."

"Why not?"

"Because...just...sit tight. You trust me, right?"

"Of course. You're the wisest person I know."

"Good." Wei winks and walks away. *This is weird, but alright.* I awkwardly look around in silence. The Athletics Center is massive. I stare at the ceiling lights and get the weirdest sense of déjà vu.

"Something about this scene seems vaguely familiar." My head snaps forward because I know that voice as well as I know my mother's.

"Omar!" My jaw drops as I spot the love of my life. He's wearing a red suit, just like he did that fateful

Thanksgiving night. I haven't seen him in person in weeks, so hearing his voice feels like taking a breath after being underwater for days.

"Last time we were here, I made you drop a cake all over yourself."

I sniff, my eyes starting to sting. "I'm not so afraid of touch anymore thanks to this jock who helped me." I meet him across the floor and fling myself into his arms. After hugging him hard, I pull back and place a warm kiss on his face. He tastes as sweet as he did the first time, and I know for certain I'll never get tired of his mouth on mine.

"What are you doing here?"

"I came to visit my boyfriend, silly." He grins, and I absolutely melt. "I've missed you like crazy."

"I've missed you too, Alligator." I can't help leaning in to kiss him multiple times while we talk. "How'd you know I was here?"

"Logan filled me in on his little plan. You know he called me freaking out? He actually thought Wei would say 'no' to him when he popped the question. Can you believe it?"

I laugh despite the tears coming down my face. God, I've needed him back in my arms. "So...are we...have you re-evaluated whether you want to keep this going? Our relationship?"

He smiles and looks up, hands in his pockets. He walks backward toward where the dance floor was. "Do you remember last year at the formal? I really wanted to ask you out."

I chuckle and wipe away a tear. "How could I forget? You came over and we slow danced anyway."

"While I'm not a student athlete anymore..." He

reaches his left hand toward me and the lights go dim. "I wanted to know if I could have this dance. On a proper dance floor this time."

Music starts to play and I assume Logan is controlling the sound system. I smile and end up in Omar's arms, swaying to the song he played for me last year.

"This really does feel like the movies," I mutter, resting my head on Omar's shoulder.

"That's kind of the point, Sylvester. With you, it's always just like the movies."

I pull back and look at his perfect face, searching for the answers.

"Sly, being apart from you…it kills me."

"Omar, I refuse to let you give up your dreams. I don't want to be another distraction, so if you feel we need to take a break—"

"No!" He chuckles and rolls his eyes. "I drove all the way here after work to tell you I love you. There's nothing to re-evaluate. You tell me not to get distracted from my dreams, but this, right here, is my dream. I want us to be together, babe."

I laugh despite myself. "I want that, too."

"I'm sorry being apart sucks, but I don't want anyone else." He pulls me close again. "Sly, you…are incredible. Because you did the impossible."

"What's that?"

"You locked down the biggest fuckboy on the soccer team." We both chuckle as we continue to slow dance. "You made me believe in romance and love again when I thought that part of my heart had died. Baby, I love you. You made me whole again."

I wipe away a tear from his face. "You make me feel whole

too, Omar."

We dance for a few more minutes, savoring every moment we have together before he has to drive back to New York City. I don't think I mind too much anymore–my heart belongs to him, so I'll find a way back every time.

Epilogue: Omar

Aggie taps the microphone and starts her announcement. "Alright all you unmarried folks, it's time for the bouquet toss!" People scramble onto the dancefloor of the banquet hall, but I just sit back with a drink in my hand, enjoying the scene. It's been eight months since Logan proposed to Wei, and now we are all back together for their wedding. "Ooh, wait, I gotta get in on this," Aggie mutters loudly. She puts the mic back on the stand and strides in front of the crowd of wedding guests.

The grooms, Wei and Logan, both sit in chairs facing away from everyone, and little Galen hands them the bouquet. The crowd counts to three, and they toss the flowers back. I see Stacia, Ravi, and Dane, along with six other folks, desperately reach up to try to catch it. They're all disappointed when a massive blond dude easily snatches it several feet above everyone's heads.

"My man is a basketball player!" Dominic Suarez, Steven's buddy from KU, walks by cheering. He walks up to the tall guy, Landon's brother Link, who kisses him on the cheek and gives him the flowers. I whoop and holler along with most of the crowd. What a cute couple.

"My brother and Dominic. I don't know if I'll ever get used to that." Landon sits next to me, nursing a drink. "Why didn't you go up there for the bouquet toss? You know if you catch it, legend says you're next to get married."

"I'm familiar with the ritual, *Landee*," I say with a grin. He chuckles, and I swirl the ice cubes in my glass. "I was feeling lazy. Why didn't *you* go up?"

"Dane went up for the both of us, but I had a feeling Link was just going to get it with his basketball powers."

I smile and look around. Ravi and Steven are at the bar chatting with Link and Dominic. Dane is talking to Wei and Logan near the dance floor. I spy Kareem and Stacia talking to little Galen and his mom, Wei's sister. Everyone's dressed to the nines, and the whole ceremony was so romantic that I may have cried during their vows.

Everything about this wedding is perfect, but I can't seem to find my hot date.

After Sly graduated, he got accepted into a social work master's program. It's not too far from my school in Manhattan, which we couldn't be happier about. As of three weeks ago, he moved in with me. It took some time getting used to living together; Sly is much more particular with cleaning than I am, and he asks me to wash surfaces way more often than I'd prefer. But having him in my arms every night is worth it. Now that we're building a home together, it feels like all the things I've ever needed in life are coming together.

I love him to death, but I'm wondering where he is right now.

"Attention, everyone." I hear his gorgeous voice, and

everyone turns to the stage where he's holding the microphone. *Sylvester O'Rourke, what are you up to?*

"This song is a gift for the groom and groom. I dedicate this to Wei, the guy who helped me discover who I really am, and Logan, the man who makes him happier than anyone." There's a smattering of awws throughout the banquet hall. "It's an old classic, and I also dedicate it to everyone who makes someone else feel complete." He looks directly at me and I get goosebumps. "If you find a love like Logan and Wei's, cherish it. This is 'You Make Me Feel Brand New' by the Stylistics."

The track starts, and Sly's booming baritone voice echoes through the room. Pretty soon, Wei and Logan, Ravi and Steven, Dominic and Link, Dane and Landon, and several other couples start slow dancing. I don't join them. I'm too transfixed by the perfect man singing on stage. My man.

Once he's done, a pop track plays and everyone disperses to their tables. Sly walks right off the stage and directly into my arms. "That was incredible!"

"Thanks, Alligator." We kiss, and my heart lights up like it did the day we kissed for the first time.

"You're chock full of surprises, aren't you?"

"Well, I picked that song for you. For us." His face goes serious, and it feels like no one else is in the room. "Before you, I thought I was broken because I never wanted anyone. I played the role of a straight guy comfortable in his skin, even though I hated being touched. But with you, I love it all. You're the exception. You always have been. Like the song says, you taught me how to live, and I'm a new man because of you."

"You always had it in you, babe." I smile and put my hands on either side of his face. "You were never broken.

You're just gray-ace, and that's perfect because I love every part of you."

He smiles and nods. "I love you, too. Omar...I want to watch cheesy rom-coms with you for decades to come. I want to fall asleep in your arms and wake you up with hand jobs. I want us to have breakfast, and I'll buy you all the chive-cream-cheese-raisin-bagels you want even though they're gross. I want all of you for years to come. What I'm trying to say is...I don't know if I ever want to get married like Logan and Wei, but...you're all I'm ever going to want. No one else."

I gasp. "Really?" I whisper, knowing full well what he's implying.

"Yes. We're not in college anymore. But I know for certain I want to spend my life with you, Omar Odom."

I kiss him firmly, then embrace him, right there in front of everyone. "I'm never going to feel this way about anyone else," I mutter into his neck. "I don't care if you never want to have sex, because *you* are the most important thing in my life."

He pulls back, his eyes shimmering. "Well then I guess you're stuck with me now, Alligator."

We both chuckle, and I put my lips on his, despite his brother and all our friends being around. Steven will need to get used to me being in his life, because I'm making Sly O'Rourke a permanent fixture in mine.

Series Epilogue: Sly

The sun shines over the massive park where we've all gathered on this breezy summer day. There are a dozen or so families roaming about, but we're at the largest picnic area laced with kids' party decorations. I'm sitting across from Landon and holding a beer in one hand and a hot dog in the other. My boyfriend jogs over, holding a massive tray of veggie burgers, and plops down right next to me.

"Okay, okay, I'm back," Omar says. "What happened next?"

"So, where was I?" Landon eats some potato chips, then wipes his mouth on the back of his hand. "Oh right, so Dane just finished this amazing ensemble number. He knows I'm sitting in the front row, so they turn the spotlight on me."

"No way," I say.

"Yes! And Dane hops down and makes a whole

speech about wanting to love me forever. Then, in front of hundreds of people in the theater, he gets on one knee."

"Aww," Omar and I coo in unison.

"I'm still shook." Landon smiles and pulls up his left hand to reveal a gold band. "Check it out!"

"Wow," Omar mutters while we both stare at it.

"You're still telling them the story, my dear fiancé?" Dane walks over with Link and Dominic in tow.

"I needed to set the scene! Now they know how you're going to make an honest man out of me." Landon pecks Dane on the cheek, and it's disgustingly cute.

"We had the privilege of being there that night," Link remarks.

"And taking *alllll* the pictures," Dominic adds. "The waterworks from this one, let me tell you!" He points to Landon, and we laugh.

"What did you expect? I got engaged!" Landon shrugs.

"You cried more at our wedding than *we* did," Link says, putting his arm around Dominic.

"I thought *we* were the suckers for romance movies," Omar says, knocking my shoulder. This earns us another roar of laughter.

I feel a vibration in my phone and check the recent text. I look around to see if they've arrived; I notice some of what I assume are Kareem's and Stacia's respective families. There are blue balloons with the number one floating around, along with trays of delicious food. Finally, around the massive picnic pavilion, I spot them walking up to us with massive blue bags in hand.

"Ravi!" I shout and wave.

"Steven!" Omar adds.

Our whole table cheers, and we get up and hug them. Landon and Omar act like they don't get together every summer and have a very active group chat with Kareem and Ravi. For the past few years, most of us have physically gone our separate ways with different career paths, but we can never stay away for too long—we're family, after all.

"Let me see the ring," Steven says, sitting next to Landon and we all chuckle.

"Alright, Dominic, we're here. You wanna tell them?" Ravi asks, sitting next to Link.

"Tell us what?" I ask.

Dom and Link look at each other, then at us. "Ravi and Steven wanted to know...the process to start a family. Because they want to adopt, just like us," Dominic says.

"Wait, what?" Dane asks. "I knew you two old married dudes were considering kids." He points to Ravi and Steven, now sitting across from each other. "But Link...you guys are thinking about adopting?"

"We...are finishing up the paperwork. We *are* adopting." Link winces and shrugs. "Uh...surprise?"

We all immediately turn to Landon, whose jaw has dropped. "Seriously?" Landon asks.

"We want to start a family. And since you boys are our family, we wanted to tell you all in person," Link says.

"That's...amazing! I'm gonna be an uncle! Again!" Landon gets up and hugs Dominic and Link and we all cheer.

"Hey, we already are uncles, remember? We're the best queer uncles ever in the history of queer uncles," Omar announces. "That's why we're all here. Where are the little ones, anyway?"

"Hey, boys!" Kareem is walking up to us with a stroller in

tow. In it rides his twins, Russell and Dustin, who just turned one. Stacia is not far behind him, toting a large diaper bag. "Sorry we took so long."

"There was a poopy emergency," Stacia says. She hugs Ravi and Steven.

"That's what *you* have to look forward to," I remark, pointing my beer bottle at Link.

"I think I'm game," Link says, putting his arm around Dominic.

"With you, I'm always game," Dom replies, smiling.

I swear, they stare at each other like they've just started dating, not like a couple who've been married for almost two years.

After eating, we take about a million photos of the twins near the cake—but never actually touching it, lest they get dirty before the end of the day—then it's time to open up the presents. Kareem and Stacia went all out for their sons, and so many family members came through, bringing gift after gift. Omar and I do the pragmatic thing and give their parents a few hundred dollars in gift cards to pay for cleaning supplies.

Once the twins are done tearing open their presents and the gift-wrapping has been cleared away, Omar and I sit down with the toddlers on a large blanket lined with pillows. Stacia is seated nearby while we play with whatever toys they have in front of them.

"And this one's Russell?" Omar asks, handing the little one a small basketball.

"Yup," Stacia says, smiling fondly. "That's Rusty. His head's a bit bigger and he looks more like Kareem, I think."

"Then this one's Dustin!" I say, putting the plastic toy

guitar in his hands.

"That's our Dusty," Stacia says. "He loves musical toys, so I need to thank Landee and Dane for getting him that." Dusty smacks the guitar buttons, and the whole thing lights up with sounds. We share a smile, and he continues to play. To my surprise, he's actually starting to make musical patterns.

"We got a future Jonas Brother over here!" I say. "We should get him to take classes with Wei!"

Stacia and I laugh, then I turn to see Omar bouncing the ball to Rusty. Rusty bounces it, and, remarkably, it actually has enough force to make it back to Omar.

Omar stands up and grins. "Rusty's got an arm!"

"Yeah, they may only be one, but they're already so different," Stacia remarks.

Omar laughs and hands the ball to Dusty, who frowns and crawls back to his mom. "Well, in our experience, artists and athletes always find a way to get along."

Omar looks at me, and I'm taken aback by how handsome he is. I swear, he hasn't aged a day in the past six years. We have our arguments, like all couples, but overall, we get along so well. He has never pressured me into having more sex than I want, and I thank God every night I decided to audition for that play. Otherwise, I might never have found my soul mate, the only man who makes my gray-asexual heart light on fire.

A few minutes later, the twins are put down for a nap and Kareem undoes his tie, which can only mean one thing: he's ready to play a friendly soccer game with his boys. We walk to the adjacent field where Landon is setting up cones as goals. I sit down on the side, expecting to watch with Dane and my brother as usual. To my surprise, Omar sits next to me.

"Aren't you gonna go play with the guys?"

"Meh, I wasn't quite up to it today. I'd rather sit here and spectate with you." I feel my face get warm as he puts his hand on my knee. I look over to see Steven on one side and Dane on the other team—that's new!

"Eh, what the hell." I turn to my left to see Dominic taking off his blazer and running up and high-fiving Ravi.

We watch our friends play their favorite game. It's a riot watching Steven smack talk Ravi since they're on opposite teams, but everyone's laughing and having a good time. Link is cheering on both sides since his brother and husband are in opposition, and it's adorable.

I think about how most of my friends on the field are starting families soon. I turn to my right to see Omar's beautiful face as the summer sun makes him glow. "What?" he asks.

"Babe, I..." I bite my lip and look down. "I know I said I didn't want to get married like my brother because it's just a piece of paper and a label, but..." I look back at his gorgeous brown eyes. "Seeing the babies today and hearing about Landon's engagement...well...I think I want it all. The wedding, the rings, the house, maybe even kids if we have the money for it." I put my hand on his cheek and, to my relief, he doesn't run away screaming.

"Are you sure, Sly?" He puts his hand on mine, still holding his face.

"With you, yeah. As long as I have you, I can take on whatever life throws at us." I lean in and kiss his sweet lips. "Or at least, I can *act* like it."

"There's no faking with you, babe. You've always been 100 percent authentic; you're a kick-ass social worker, and you put up with me!" I chuckle and rub his cheek. "You're not playing the role of a romantic hero. You are one."

I smile and kiss him again. "I love you, and I wanna marry you and lock you down," I say, tears welling up.

"No need, Sylvester. You locked this Alligator down a long time ago." He pulls me in for a massive hug. "I love you too. Thank you...for making me believe in romance and love again." We pull apart and he puts his arm around me so we can both watch our friends play soccer.

I may not be totally into sex or being touched, but when Omar holds me, I always feel at home. He accepts that I'm gray-asexual, and that's more than I could have ever dreamed of. I can't wait to start the next phase of our lives, because when Omar and I are together, I know for sure romance is real.

(The End)

Thank You

Dear Reader,

Thank you for completing this book. Omar's and Sly's love story was so much fun to write. More importantly, this whole series has been rewarding— my first ever series, what?!

If you had told me before 2020 that I'd write an entire four novel romance series in under a year, I'd think you were crazy. Now here we are! I put a piece of myself in every character I write, and every romantic scene that fills your heart it brings me joy as well. Yes, I may have shed a tear or two while writing this.

What does the future hold? More romances, with racecar drivers, grief support groups, gamer nerds, and so much more. The world of Artists and Athletes is never really over — you'll see these boys in cameos, I'm sure of it. And if you ever need a pick-me-up, you can always go back to book 1 and experience all that Korham University has to offer from the very beginning. See the next page for links for past and future works of mine.

My author journey is just getting started! I hope you read along with me.

Never stop loving life and never stop reading,

CD Rachels

Acknowledgments

I wouldn't be here without my book best friend Rod. You'll always be the main reason I got into writing. Thanks to Lee Blair for being a fellow author and a good friend! The graphics are much appreciated. To Catherine and Karen and Storystylings and GRR: you made my book a reality. To all my Chill Discoursians: every interaction on my socials fills me with joy, and every private message and reviews means the world to me. It really, truly keeps me writing more and more. Being an author can be solitary at times, but with all of your chats, it's not so lonely.

Other Works

* * *

Formula Q series

Get ready to burn rubber and take pole. Look out for the new motorsports romance novel "Drive to Thrive."

About the Author

About the Author

CD Rachels has been coming up with stories since he was little. At first it was all about superheroes and pocket monsters, but his genre of choice has expanded since puberty.

He's been consuming young adult gay fiction since he was a teen, but within the past five years, he's moved up to the big leagues of gay adult romance. In 2020 during quarantine, he burned through more male/male romance books than he ever had in the previous 29 years combined.

He lives in New York City with the love of his life and works in health insurance. When he's not reading and writing, he's playing board games and practicing music. He is honored to become a published author, and if you're reading this, your support means so much to him that he has goosebumps just thinking about it.

Be the first to hear about all his updates and new releases!

Sign up for his newsletter "The Chill Discourse Report"

Follow him on Instagram: @cdrachels

Join his Facebook group where he hosts polls and chats with readers nonstop: "CD Rachels' Chill Discourse Room"

Follow/review his other works on Goodreads here

Check him out on BookBub too here

Made in the USA
Middletown, DE
22 August 2023